Wordsworth and Helen Maria Williams

Wordsworth and Helen Maria Williams; or, the Perils of Sensibility

Three Grasmere Essays

Richard Gravil

𝓗𝓔𝓑 ☼ Humanities-Ebooks, 2010

First published by *Humanities-Ebooks, LLP,*
Tirril Hall, Tirril, Penrith CA10 2JE

The Ebook (with the facility of word and phrase search) is available as a pdf from http://www.humanities-ebooks.co.uk or to libraries from Ebrary, and with abridged appendices in Kindle format.

ISBN 978-1-84760-094-3 Ebook
ISBN 978-1-84760-095-0 Paperback

For Fiona

Helen Maria Williams, by Ozias Humphrey, 1792

Contents

Preface

The chapters in this volume are developed from lectures given at the Wordsworth Summer Conference and Winter School in 2007 and 2008. The talks were not initially conceived as a series, and the three chapters might have appeared in any order. It would have made sense to begin with Helen Maria Williams's earliest influence on William Wordsworth, then look in detail at the relationship between their accounts of the French Revolution, and close by glancing at the damage done to his critical reputation by his *liaison dangereux* with feminine sensibility as demonstrated in *Poems in Two Volumes*. Or I could have opened with the celebrated matter of Jeffrey's handling of both *Lyrical Ballads* and the *Poems in Two Volumes* and then considered what it was in Wordsworth's poetic allegiances that tempted him to betray so much 'feminine' sensibility in his 'Pansies' as one might call them, and why the impact of so much sensibility had the effect of thrusting the admitted 'manliness' of the political sonnets into the background.

It seemed, on balance, best to open with the grand historical topos of 'human nature seeming born again', as encountered first by a female historian and then a male poet; then to examine other traces of the former's work and sensibility to be found in the latter; and to conclude (with what was, in fact, the first lecture) by wondering whether it was these traces of 'feminine' sensibility, or 'effeminacy', by the standards of the day, that drew down upon one hapless lake poet the scorn of Edinburgh. Complete reconstruction of the approach in the first two chapters proved to be beyond my skill, so the chapters do treat some elements of the story of Wordsworth and Williams, especially as regards their experience of France, twice over, though with different emphases.

The package is, to my mind, held together by this matter of (as I would have it) ungendered poetic sensibility. Apart from anything of value that I might be found to be saying about Wordsworth and Williams, or indeed Wordsworth and Jeffrey, the one thing I would most like to register is the wrong-headedness of Coleridge's famous assertion that Wordsworth's personality was entirely masculine— that there was nothing feminine in his nature.

Parts of chapter 1 are making their fourth appearance. A version of it was published in *The Wordsworth Circle*, 40:1 (Winter 2009), and in it I drew on an article first published in 1989, in the French Revolution volume of the *Yearbook of English Studies*, edited by J. R. Watson, which Stephen Gill has also seen fit to resurrect in his Oxford 'Casebooks in Criticism' collection on *The Prelude* (2006). But I have avoided the temptation to draw too much upon a relevant chapter on '"The Milder day": or, Manliness and Minstrelsy' in *Wordsworth's Bardic Vocation* (2003).

Introduction: Williams and Wordsworth, an Odyssey

While still a schoolboy, William Wordsworth, as most Wordsworthians know, was already somewhat enamoured of Helen Maria Williams. He expressed his admiration for the poet and her sensibility in his first published poem—*Sonnet on seeing Miss Helen Maria Williams weep at a tale of distress*—on which poem and its significance, I will dilate briefly in Chapter 2. Their stories are considerably more intertwined than that, however. This little book will argue that Williams's work had a greater influence on Wordsworth's poetical development than she is generally given credit for, and that Wordsworth's loyalty to the kind of writing her *Poems in Two Volumes* (1786) helped to inspire in him is one of the primary reasons for the acrimonious reception of his own *Poems, in Two Volumes* (1807). It will also claim that her work is a major, if not the major, influence on the great poem of the nineteenth century, *The Prelude*. In short, while this book has no discoveries to announce about their connections, it does seek to re-assess the significance of Williams to Wordsworth, both as a poet of the Age of Sensibility, and as a writer of a compendious eye-witness history of the great event of the age, an event formative in both of their lives.

On 13 July 1790, as *all* Wordsworthians know, Wordsworth and Robert Jones arrived in Calais 'on the eve of that great federal day', the festival that was to mark the first anniversary of the French Revolution. Helen Maria Williams, on that day, was already in Paris. Indeed she had a grand-stand seat in the Champ de Mars, to witness what she called 'the most sublime spectacle which, perhaps, was ever represented on the theatre of this earth'. Her description of Louis XIV and 600,000 spectators saying the national oath together begins the first of some fifteen volumes of contemporary history, volumes that would be cannibalized repeatedly, in the three

'French' books of *The Prelude*, in Carlyle's magnificent account of *The French Revolution*, in Felicia Hemans's poetry (especially in her poem 'Prisoners' Evening Service' based on Williams's own imprisonment in Paris), and in Dickens's *A Tale of Two Cities*. To a very large extent the defining images that stand for the French Revolution in English culture are hers.

Like Wordsworth, pocketing a stone of the Bastille, or viewing the scenes of the September massacres, Williams looks on events in her first volume (*Letters Written in France, in the Summer 1790*) partly as a tourist, conscious of her inexperience and very candid about the emotional nature of her responses, positive and negative, to events as they unfold. She is shown, for instance, 'the far-famed lanterne' at which, for want of a gallows, the first victims of popular fury [after the liberation of the Bastille] were executed, and comments 'I own that the sight of la lanterne chilled the blood within my veins'. But immediately she takes on the mantle of apologist that will remain with her for the rest of her career: 'alas! where do the records of history point out a revolution unstained by some actions of barbarity?' (*Letters from France*, Series 1, Volume 1, page 80).

Williams's first volume of *Letters* was published just two weeks after Edmund Burke's famous *Reflections on the Revolution in France*—and although her contribution to the revolution debate is rarely mentioned nowadays (those of Price, Paine and Wollstonecraft being much better known) it was much celebrated at the time. This is shown in an anonymous cartoon (reproduced on the next page) entitled 'Don Dismallo running the Literary Gauntlet'. It shows Burke, dressed as a clown (for mistaking the true significance of events in France), being flogged first by Helen Maria Williams, and only then by Richard Price, Mrs Barbauld, Sheridan, three allegorical figures, Horne Tooke and the Whig historian Catherine Macaulay [Mrs Graham]. Williams is first not because of her eminence at the time but because her quite accidental riposte (she knew nothing, of course, of Burke's imminent *Reflections* while writing her first volume) happens to have appeared first.

In the Autumn of 1790, Wordsworth returned to Cambridge to finish his degree. There he almost certainly read the first instalment

Don Dismallo Running the Literary Gauntlet

of *Letters from France*, which Williams had returned to England to publish. In this volume, *Letters written in France, in the Summer of 1790, to a Friend in England; containing Various Anecdotes relative to the French revolution; and memoirs of Mons. and Madame du F—* (London: T Cadell, 1790), Wordsworth later found the basis of the tale of 'Vaudracour and Julia' in *The Prelude* of 1805.

In August 1791 Williams returned to France, announcing her trial emigration in a remarkable poem *A Farewell for 2 Years, to England* (1791) on which the *Analytical* wrote that 'The idea of visiting France, now become the first seat of freedom, fires her muse with more than usual ardour'. Whether Wordsworth was inspired by her poem or by the *Letters* to follow her to France for his own much longer second visit, his 'Residence in France', is not clear, but follow her he did, in November 1791. With a letter of introduction in his pocket (from Charlotte Smith) he made first for Dieppe, then Rouen, then Orleans—following Williams's own route. One might almost say he stalked her—but he finally missed her altogether, arriving in Orleans shortly after she left.

'The circumstance' he wrote to his brother Richard, 'was a considerable disappointment to me' (*EY* 69). It is to me, also. As we know, Wordsworth made his own connections in France, but he did not, like Williams, visit the Jacobins in the company of Mme Roland, or take part in the constitutional councils of the Girondins, which, with the patronage of the well-connected poetess he might well have done. *He* knew of the bravery and the significance of Jean-Baptiste Louvet primarily from Louvet's writings: *she* knew him as a member of her circle. Nor would membership of her society have been at all improbable had Wordsworth been in the right place at the right time. Among Williams's friends and occasional callers at her famous salons—though mostly in the early 1800s when she and John Hurford Stone were very comfortably off in their Parisian 'hotel'— were Wordsworth's most admired English politician, Charles James Fox; his Somerset neighbour, Tom Poole; his great friend and travelling companion of later years, Henry Crabb Robinson; the anti-slavery campaigners Thomas and Catherine Clarkson of Eusemere; and one of his heroes of national independence, Taddeusz Kosciuszki.

Williams took a two-month break in England in June 1792, while Wordsworth was amorously entangled in Blois, to publish her second book of *Letters from France* (George Robinson, 1792), in which she made the famous remark that 'living in France at present, appears to me somewhat like living in a region of romance' (1.2.4). THis is the very image that Wordsworth would use to encapsulate both his own perceptions and of those of his guide and hero, Michel Beaupuy. Wordsworth's return to England took place in December 1792; Williams decided very bravely to stay in France after war was declared, and lost much of her public by doing so. Charlotte Smith was writing her Royalist apologetics in *The Emigrants*, about a king 'whose only crime / Was being born a monarch'.[1] Anna Seward appealed to Williams publicly in the *Gentleman's Magazine* of February 1793 to leave that 'land of carnage!' rather than risk perpetual alienation from her country. But as we know from Wordsworth's history at his time you don't have to leave your country to be alienated from it: you can sit in country churches listening to prayers for national victory while rejoicing quietly at national defeats.

Her alienation, however, lasted rather longer than his. For a while, at the height of the Terror, following imprisonment in Paris in October–November 1793 (when Wordsworth most probably did *not* make his legendary attempt to reach Orleans and rescue Annette Vallon), Williams took refuge in Switzerland,. There she composed the first volume of her second series of *Letters*, and also wrote a realistic corrective to Wordsworth's somewhat idealized views of that country. But she returned to Paris, after the fall of Robespierre—a major epoch in the lives of both poets, in whose treatments of the event there are conspicuous imagistic parallels and almost identical feelings—to work on the volumes about Robespierre's Terror. The two volumes of *Letters Containing a Sketch of the Politics of France from the thirty-first of May 1793 to the twenty-eighth of July 1794 and of the Scenes which have passed in the Prisons of Paris* (vols 1 and 2 of the second series of Letters; vols 5 and 6 of the whole), were

---

1   *The Emigrants* (1793) 2: 54–5. Williams writes in Letters 1.4.9 that 'History will indeed condemn Lewis the sixteenth. The evidence of his guilt [inviting foreign armies to war on his people, and organising a system of bribery and corruption] is clear.

published in London in July 1795, taken to Racedown by Azaziah Pinney, and read by the Wordsworths early in 1796.

Williams's commitment to France did not mean that she cared any less than Wordsworth did about the successive betrayals of the revolution, first by Robespierre and then by Napoleon. She wrote quite as ferociously as he did about Napoleon's assumption of the Consulate and the Imperial purple, and such continued sympathies no doubt facilitated the meeting of minds when the poets finally met, for the first time in their long and mostly one-sided relationship, in Paris in 1820. William and Dorothy spent two evenings in her company. Williams had already been sent Wordsworth's volume of Waterloo odes, by Henry Crabb Robinson. Wordsworth recited, from memory, Williams's 1790 *Sonnet to Hope.* After the meeting, Dorothy solicited, via Crabb Robinson, a copy of her 1819 *Letters on the Events which have passed in France since the restoration in 1815.*

Such is the outline. The intellectual and emotional affinities run much deeper, and they account, it seems to me for some of the chorus of disapproval that descended upon Wordsworth when, in 1807, he offered the world a volume of poems that is notable for many things, but most of all for its loyalty to the values entailed in Miss Williams's brand of Sensibility.

1. Wordsworth's Revolutionary Anima

> 'Living in France appears to me somewhat like living in a region
> of romance … and while I contemplate these things I sometimes
> think that the age of chivalry, instead of being past for ever, is
> just returned'
>
> —Helen Maria Williams

> 'Moi je m'en vais dans l'Elysee,
> Avec Sydney m'entretenir'
>
> —Jean-Baptiste Louvet

'A Region of Romance'

The voice of *The Prelude*, Anthony Harding argued some years ago
at the Wordsworth Summer Conference, is a palimpsest; not egotistical, as too often supposed, but representative. In this respect, it
seems to me, the three great poetic voices of the nineteenth century,
Wordsworth, Tennyson and Whitman, are triplets. Each might have
claimed, as Tennyson did of *In Memoriam*, that the 'I' of the poem
is not that of the author, but 'the voice of the human race' speaking
through him. In this chapter I revisit a previous treatment of the frac-
tured 'voice' of books 9 and 10 of *The Prelude*, correcting an essay
I wrote for the 1989 *Yearbook of English Studies*. In Book 2 of *The
Prelude*, Wordsworth famously finds such 'self-presence' of the past
that 'often do I seem / Two consciousnesses, conscious of myself
and of some other Being' (1850, 2: 27–33). Hence my 1989 title:
'"Some other Being": Wordsworth in *The Prelude*'. What creates the
difficulty for the reader of the *Prelude*'s revolutionary triad, I argued

then, is the 'self-presence', alongside the autobiographer, of an *alter ego* who is capable of thrusting aside whatever attempts Wordsworth may make to sustain a tone of apologetics. This *alter ego* is related to those other manifestations of Wordsworth's revolutionary persona, the Solitary of *The Excursion* and Oswald in *The Borderers*, in whose mouths Wordsworth places many of his own best lines.

But perhaps it is more complicated than that. Since *The Prelude* is not simply an autobiography, with its inevitable conflicts between selves diachronically understood, but the narrative of a representative mind, and a portrait of the age, perhaps the self presented is more properly perceived as a lamination. One example of how the personal and impersonal may coalesce, arises in an exciting suggestion by Kenneth Johnston. Johnston speculates that in the curious *Prelude* manuscript reference to 'anguish fugitive in woods, in caves concealed' (de Selincourt *Prelude*, p. 580) we may catch sight of Wordsworth's daring journey through the Vendée, in October 1793, meeting up with Gorsas and Louvet in Caen, to visit Annette Vallon.[1] It is far likelier, however, that such a desperate adventure (the only evidence for which is Carlyle's possible misconception that Wordsworth had witnessed the execution of Gorsas) did *not* take place, and that in writing *The Prelude* Wordsworth was remembering a book he read in 1795, namely Jean-Baptiste Louvet's *Narrative of the Dangers to which I have been exposed, since the 31st of May, 1793*. This book is notable for its vigorously partisan account of Jacobin politics and for its immensely exciting narrative of flight through Brittany and the Gironde, through hedges, ditches and meadows, in constant fear of detection or betrayal, before taking refuge in the caverns of Mount Jura—literally 'in caves concealed'—where, between 19 April and 22 July 1794, Louvet wrote his *Narrative* (237).

So, while Wordsworth's 'France' is partly his own, it is also an attempt to render the experience of an age, and especially of all 'ingenuous youth'. Perhaps—like Whitman's *Song of Myself* which is also the song of America—it is more, not less, authentic if its tissues derive from the public domain—from, most especially, Louvet,

---

1   Kenneth R. Johnston, *The Hidden Wordsworth: Poet, Lover, Rebel, Spy* (1998), 392.

whose *Narrative* was published by Joseph Johnson (Wordsworth's own publisher) in 1795; from Catherine Macaulay's *Observations on Burke's Reflections;* from such radical as George Dyer, Gilbert Wakefield and William Frend; from David Williams, the most eminent Welshman in the councils of the early republic; from numerous accounts of the French Revolution in named and anonymous English publications on the subject, and from Mary Wollstonecraft's rarely quoted *An Historical and Moral View of the French Revolution* (1795).

But most of all, I have no doubt, he learned from his teenage poetic heart-throb and revolutionary *anima*, Helen Maria Williams in her *Letters from France.* Indeed if there ever was a conclusive instance of the male writer absorbing the female, incorporating her tropes into his own, it is this strangely unsung instance of the use he clearly made of the work of this 'scribbling trollop' and 'intemperate advocate of Gallic licentiousness' as contemporaries called her.[1] So I want to correct my 1989 sense of Wordsworthian solipsism. When I hinted at this correction in the preface to *Wordsworth's Bardic Vocation* (2003), Duncan Wu, in a generous review of that book, took exception to my charge that Wordsworth extensively 'plagiarised' Helen Maria Williams in his account of revolutionary France. So let me rephrase the claim, or enlarge upon it.

At the time he began to write *The Prelude*, with a primary aim of addressing those who in consequence of 'the complete failure of the French Revolution'—in Coleridge's estimation—had lost their faith in human progress, Wordsworth had had some, but perhaps insufficient experience of that revolution. He had arrived in Calais in 1790 at almost the same moment that Helen Maria Williams arrived in Paris (13 July) and during his subsequent residence in France, as he points out, he missed the September massacres 'by one short month'. Moreover, he missed, entirely, the course of the Great Terror itself,

---

1   According to Janet Todd, in her facsimile collection of the letters (Delmar, 1975), Horace Walpole described her as the former and the Reverend Richard Polwhele as the latter. I am, like any other recent convert to Helen Maria Williams, greatly indebted to Deborah Kennedy's invaluable *Helen Maria Williams and the Age of Revolution* (London: Associated University Presses, 2002) for almost all of my information on her life.

except vicariously, through what he might have read, or (as Nicholas Roe has argued)[1] what he might have known or imagined of the perils undergone by Annette Vallon's family at the hands of people who—like himself—thought that in the 'dog-day heat' of revolution a little blood-shedding is par for the course. Bluntly, he is unable to write an eye-witness account of the Terror because *he wasn't there*. In authoring a historically plausible account of the course of a revolution and its impact upon a representative (if somewhat androgynous) English sensibility he had no serious option but to rely, as Carlyle and Dickens did, also, on the most authoritative inside account of how that Revolution had developed, and it so happens that that account is Helen Maria's.

It is generally accepted that Wordsworth read at least the 1790 and 1795 instalments of *Letters from France*—that is, four volumes of the eight.[2] The first volume—*Letters written in France, in the Summer of 1790, to a Friend in England*—was widely available in France during his residence there, even if he did not read it in England. By the 1795 'instalment', I mean the account of the Jacobin Terror, from the infamous proscription of the Girondin deputies to the execution of Robespierre, in *Letters Containing a Sketch of the Politics of France from the thirty-first of May 1793, till the twenty-eighth of July 1794* (2 vols, 1795). He had access to these volumes through Azaziah Pinney, in Racedown. And as Duncan Wu points out, the *Weekly Entertainer* (*sic*) carried extracts from the prison scenes in September and October 1795, shortly before Wordsworth also read Louvet's *Narrative*.

What we know, also, though it is not usually put in quite this way, is that Williams and Wordsworth belonged—certainly in the 1790s, before the advent of Napoleon briefly divided them—to a closely knit group of politically motivated 'friends of liberty', a *coterie*, between

---

1   'Politics, History and Wordsworth's Poems', in Stephen Gill, ed., *The Cambridge Companion to Wordsworth* (2003) 196–212.

2   It would be very surprising if he did not at some point read all eight volumes of *Letters*, and indeed the *Tour in Switzerland*, the *Sketches*, and the later volumes narrating Napoleon's 100 days and assessing the Bourbon restoration. It seems, these days, to be widely assumed that if a book does not appear in either volume of Duncan Wu's *Wordsworth's Reading*, Wordsworth did not read it. The only legitimate inference is that we have no documentary proof that he did.

whom there was an iceberg of networking, which is to say, a visible
and documented degree of communication suggestive of an invisible
but considerably more extensive web of relations. Both were admirers of four leading republicans: the Abbé Grégoire, Bishop of Blois,
who (as Nicholas Roe pointed out in *The Radical Years*) forced the
pace on the declaration of a republic and the impeachment of the
king; Gorsas and Brissot, who were among the first so-called moderates to be guillotined; and Jean-Baptiste Louvet, who survived the
terror to become president of the National Convention (and one of
The Prelude's select band of named heroes). Both identified thoroughly with the leading advocates of Commonwealth politics, and
with those in France who shared that allegiance.

Before I go on, I should perhaps remark on an oddity of recent
historical scholarship, a tendency to refer to the political values of
late eighteenth century Commonwealthmen—campaigners like
Major John Cartwright—as somewhat anachronistic and by implication 'liberal' rather than 'revolutionary' in the contemporary scene.
Romanticists are familiar with this famous moment, celebrated by
Williams in her second volume:

> I was at the Jacobins when the English, French and American col-
> ours, fastened together with bands of laurel and national ribbon
> were placed in the hall… from every quarter were re-echoed the
> cries of "Vive la Liberté—Vive l'Angleterre—Vive la France—
> Vives les nations libres!" … It was proposed by some of the
> members, and ordered by the society, that the busts of Price,
> Franklin, Algernon Sidney, Jean-Jaques Rousseau … should be
> placed beneath the banners of the three nations. …The names of
> Milton, of Locke and of Hambden re-echoed through the hall….
> (*Letters,* 1.2.112–3)

Is it really 'anachronistic' in this revolutionary moment to cite
Sidney? Louvet's wonderful *Narrative* provides not only one of the
most significant corollaries to Helen Maria's interpretation of the
revolution, but a moving gloss on this use of Sidney's name as a
talisman. Expecting arrest and execution at any moment as he tra-
versed France, hiding in hayricks and disguised as a peasant woman,
Louvet narrates how in 1793 he solemnly composed what he calls

his 'Hymn to Death' which ends: 'Moi je m'en vais dans l'Elysee, / Avec Sydney m'entretenir'[1] Later he narrates how the deputy editor of Brissot's newspaper, the *Patriote Francais*, the 23 year old Girey-Dupré, chants his own 'death-song' praising Brissot who preceded him to the guillotine on 31 October, 1793: 'Yes; I loved him: yes; I respect, and I admire him. Like Aristides he lived, like Sydney he died: I have no wish but to share his fate!' (*Narrative*, 213).

To understand the vibrations of Commonwealthmanship in Louvet's *Narrative* or Wordsworth's sonnets or Williams's *Letters*, one needs to go back to the decade of Wordsworth's birth. In England the 1770s, either side of the Thomas Jefferson's 'Declaration of Independence'—which, with the aid of Tom Paine, effected a revolution far more durable than the French—saw much pamphleteering and agitation, inside parliament and out, for constitutional renovation. In 1780 a young Charles James Fox led agitation in and around Westminster for Cartwright's remarkably Chartist programme of annual parliaments, universal male suffrage, equal electoral districts and paid MPs. For forty years, during which political progress was stalled, radical sensibilities were nurtured on a great succession of tracts demanding new rights (cannily disguised as ancient liberties)—tracts including Price's *Observations on the Nature of Civil Liberty* (1776), his *Discourse on the Love of Our Country* (1789) and Thelwall's *The Rights of Nature against the Usurpations of Establishments* (1796). The 'true Whig' critics of English constitutional decadence, the proponents of American independence and the revolution societies of the 1790s share a unitary discourse which stemmed—as Wordsworth makes clear in the sonnets—from Anglo-American republican theorists in the Age of Milton.

It is all summarized in the famous invocation, from the sonnet 'Great Men have been among us', of 'The later Sydney, Marvel, Harrington, / Young Vane and others who called Milton friend'. It is astonishing what Wordsworth can pack into six talismanic names, and the significance of Sidney, Harrington and Vane, at least, deserves

---

1   'For me I fly to Elysium, To converse with Sidney', Jean-Baptiste Louvet, *Narrative of the Dangers to which I have been exposed, since the 31st of May, 1793,*109

to be mentally unpacked each time we read those lines. Algernon Sidney is one of the great libertarian martyrs, and his *Discourses on Government* are fundamental to every strand of libertarian politics in England, France and America in the 18th Century. Executed for regicide, he died beseeching God's favour for 'that OLD CAUSE in which I was from youth engaged'[1] and lamented that he had lived to see 'the liberty which we hoped to establish oppressed ... the best of our nation made a prey to the worst ... the people enslaved [and] no man safe, but by such evil and infamous means, as flattery and bribery' (*Discourses*, xi). What he wrote about monarchy underlies Wordsworth treatment of that subject in the *Letter to the Bishop of Llandaff*: 'I doubt whether any better reason can be given, why there have been, and are more monarchies than popular governments in the world', Sidney wrote, 'than that the nations are more easily drawn into corruption than defended from it; and I think that monarchy can be said to be natural in no other sense, than that our depraved nature is most inclined to that which is worst.' According to Sidney, the Saxons (duly celebrated in Wordsworth's sonnet on the men of Kent) 'acknowledged no human laws but their own, received no kings, but such as swore to observe them, and deposed those who did not well perform their oaths and duty'. Dangerous words, even in 1802.

James Harrington was author of one of the most celebrated works of republican theory, advocating a constitutional balance between property and people. The Harringtonian republic described in *Oceana* is based upon a bicameral system (such as most of the American states and the union itself ultimately adopted), with its members elected by rotation (a third of the members being elected at any one time), a subtly graded system of property qualification for membership of the assembly and the senate, a limited franchise (such as Federalist leaders clung on to in New York and elsewhere until well into the 19th century), and a brilliant device for the separation of powers: it would be the business of his senate to elaborate policy, and of the assembly to accept or decline, after testing the public will, the senate's proposals. While *Oceana* (like the initial French *Declaration of Rights*) recognised property as a fundamental human right, Harrington, like

---

1   *Discourses on Government* (London: J Johnson, 1795), xix.

the Paine of *Agrarian Justice*, provided for a periodic redistribution of property. For Harrington the relation between property and power was fundamental to his constitutional definitions. 'If one man be sole landlord' Harrington says, 'his empire is absolute. If a few possess the land, this makes the *Gothic* or feudal constitution. If the whole people be landlords, then it is a commonwealth.'[1] It is true, of course that some Jacobins thought they could sever the relation between liberty and property, but as more or less every social experiment has shown since then, in the Soviet Union, Eastern Europe and China, and as Wordsworth's Cumbrian experience told him, there is some historical evidence that ownership—whether we like it or not—does indeed (in Thoreau's phrase) have some foundation in human nature.

And 'young Vane'? Sir Henry cut his political teeth in New England, as very youthful governor of Massachusetts. He returned to England as one of the champions of the Commonwealth, and leader of the House of Commons. It was he, in his pamphlet *A Healing Question* (1656), drawing on a faith in colonial militias, who proposed that since no other constituted authority existed, after fall of the monarchy, and since the army embodied the people in the most representative body then available, it should function as a Convention 'to debate freely, and agree upon the particulars that, by way of fundamental Constitutions, shall be laid and inviolably observed'. In effect, he invented the concept of a grand constitutional convention that remained the dream of English Jacobins and Chartists alike.

Quietly deriding the politics of anyone of the age who was inspired by such antique figures is only one of the distortions in modern critical practice. Another is an equivocation in the use of the word 'radical'. The editors of the Broadview edition of *Letters from France* (Neil Freistat and Susan Lanser) comment that in May / June 1793 'the more *radical* Jacobins ousted the more conservative Girondins' and that 'Marat's assassination in July 1793 by the Girondin sympathizer Charlotte Corday had intensified *radical* sentiment in the capital'.[2] I am not sure why one would edit a work like *Letters from*

---

1   *Oceana*, 18.
2   Neil Fraistat and Susan S Lanser, eds, *Letters Written in France in the Summer of 1790* (Peterborough, Ontario: Broadview Literary Texts, 2001) 23, 24.

France, even the not very representative first volume, if one took the view that both Williams and her allies Brissot and Louvet were 'conservative'. I want, also, to throw into doubt the conclusion reached by Fraistat and Lanser in their introduction—notwithstanding this view of their subject's supposed conservatism—that 'Where Wordsworth retreated into "transcendence", Williams remained immersed in history'.[1] It is impossible *not* to be immersed in history, and if this chapter does not bring such a conclusion into question, meditation on the parallels adduced in my appendix may do so.

Gary Kelly, who hardly ever speaks of Williams's view of the revolution without the epithet 'feminized', as in 'her feminized revolution'—as if 'her' revolution were a world away from the real one—also distances himself from her fundamental, and surely plausible view, that liberty has to have a constitutional basis in a workable system of representation. He speaks of how Williams refers to the terror as 'this revolutionary, or rather counter-revolutionary impulse' and expresses surprise that Williams '*even* [sic] compares the Jacobin leaders to … despotic rulers of antiquity.'[2] Why wouldn't she? Not only were Louvet, Brissot and his allies the most determined advocates of a republic, of the trial of the king, of war upon the monarchical powers, of exporting the revolution to the rest of Europe, and of the abolition of slavery, but the methods of their opponents—dispensing with representation, closing the press, and rule by the manipulation of a mob—undermined the only framework that could have given real and permanent effect to the revolution. The effect of their opponents' contempt for constitutional practice was, as Williams argues, *precisely* counter-revolutionary. It resulted in repeated spasms of despotic rule, first by the Mountain and subsequently by Napoleon. The more one immerses oneself in the later volumes of Williams's *Letters* the more clear it becomes that Williams does not deserve to be patronized as someone who did not really understand the issues.

Having set out my stall, which is essentially aligned with Mary Wollstonecraft's least quoted work,[3] let me restate my position as

---

1   Fraistat and Lanser, 50.
2   Gary Kelly, *Women, Writing and Revolution 1790–1827* (Oxford: Clarendon Press, 1993) 64.
3   Wollstonecraft's *Historical and Moral View of the French Revolution* argues

regard William Wordsworth and Helen Maria Williams. It would take a very long time to encapsulate what is common to Wordsworth's writing in *The Letter to the Bishop of Llandaff* and *The Prelude*, and Williams's eight volumes of *Letters from France*, her two volumes of *Sketches*, the two volumes of her *Tour in Switzerland*, and her two post restoration histories. It would take a very long time even to comment on all the parallels in my tabulation of them—some close, some distant, and by no means exhaustive (see Appendix, pp. 111–22). So I would like, rather, to sketch some of the broad and obvious parallels, and then return to look at some of the more curious highlights.

Wordsworth shares with Williams, first, the conviction, in 1790–93 especially, that the revolution has transformed humanity and inspired a condition of general happiness, a conviction so strong that neither feels obliged, as Williams puts it, to 'weep for the rich', or in Wordsworth's case, in *Llandaff*, for the princes of the church. Both feel and express ambivalence towards Catholicism, deploring it as a form of superstition, and an abettor of absolutism, while lamenting the sack of monasteries. Both bodies of work depict the revolution as a new era in the history of mankind and compare living in France, in the 1790s, to exploring 'a region of romance'. Both deplore but ultimately excuse such excesses as the September massacres, and exult—to an extraordinary degree in both cases—in French victories and English defeats. Both express, repeatedly, a conviction that the sun of liberty *was* rising, though hidden in turbulence and darkness. Both support unequivocally the declaration of a republic, and spare but a moment to reflect on the 'unhappy Monarch' as both call him. Wordsworth it seems to me, goes much further than Williams does to justify regicide, though they agree that he was indeed guilty as charged (guilty principally, like Charles I, of treason against his own people), and most certainly had to be tried. In her 4th volume she looks back on the relative extremism of Brissot and Condorcet, in the context of 1792, an extremism shared by Louvet and of course by Wordsworth, when 'Brissot argued for the king to be tried, and

---

that the fundamental failure of the French Revolution, when compared with the American, is that despite having David Williams to help them, it took the perennially theory-driven French an unconscionable time to arrive at a workable constitution.

Condorcet argued for a Republic when the consensus was still for limited monarchy' (1.4.160).

Williams, of course, argues that the real French revolution was a constitutional one, and depicts Robespierre's reign as an usurpation. Both compare Robespierre to the high priest or chief regent of 'Moloch' and exult in deeply emotional terms at the fall of Robespierre in June 1794, at which moment both express perfect confidence that the revolution will now return to its proper course. Both worry that France's wars of defence are turning into wars of aggression—though this does not shake their allegiance to those supposed 'moderates' like Brissot who first promoted the policy of exporting the revolution by force—and in both cases it is very hard indeed to tell which of France's military adventures they have qualms about (a studied or insouciant vagueness as to chronology is a feature of both *The Prelude* and the *Letters*). Despite this reservation, both believe that France may bring about the liberation of Europe, and both hope that in Wordsworth's astonishing expression (especially astonishing given that the utterance is clearly applied to *mid 1794*, after the fall of Robespierre) her victories will be 'great, universal, irresistible'.

At the close of the 1790s, both poets are dismayed by Britain's handling of the short-lived Neapolitan Republic, and regard Nelson's betrayal of the patriots of Naples as a blot on Nelson's career and on England's name (and Wordsworth, like Southey, relies upon Williams's treatment of the matter in her *Sketches of the State of Manners and Opinions in the French Republic*, 1801). Both, in 1801/02, deplore the despotism of Napoleon, and while their histories diverge on such matters as Switzerland and Spain, both writers come to welcome, eventually, both Waterloo and the restoration of the Bourbons—to such an extent that Henry Crabb Robinson, who knows both of them well, feels he can send to Helen Maria Williams Wordsworth's remarkable (and, to some, notorious) volume of poems celebrating Waterloo.

To return a little more deliberately to some of these points. Both the *Letter to the Bishop of Llandaff* and the second volume of Williams's first series of *Letters* have to deal with the initial stages of revolutionary violence, and they take very much the same stance. 'Shall we conclude, she asks [as Wordsworth asks in his *Letter to the Bishop of Llandaff*,], that 'because the fanatics of liberty have committed some detestable crimes, ... liberty is an evil?' No, she answers: 'The occasional evils which have happened in the infant state of liberty, are but the effects of despotism. Men have been long treated with inhumanity, therefore they are ferocious. They have often been betrayed, therefore they are suspicious. They have once been slaves, and therefore they are tyrants' (1.2.204). Wordsworth's equivalent utterance is in my Appendix. She reports much more circumstantially than he does on the execution of the king, on the lamentable murders of 2 September, and on Louvet's accusation of Robespierre, which relates specifically to that event. She is able to give, as he cannot, a circumstantial account of the rising power of 'the Mountain', and of how under the mob-rule of the Mountain any superiority of mind came to be 'considered as an aristocratical deviation from the great principles of equality'. Nonetheless, her sympathy remains, as does his, with France: menaced 'by a host of foes without' France's understandable suspicion excuses her ferocity. Where Wordsworth vividly compresses his sense of Pitt's ultimate responsibility for Parisian terror into a single image, 'the goaded land waxed mad', Williams sets out the causation: 'Although every person of sense and integrity in France lamented the internal disorders excited by the mountain faction, yet no man chose to receive laws imposed by Dumourier at the head of a conquering army' (1.4.67), and consequently, his domestic 'treason ... has raised the credit of Marat' (1.4.69). Her example may explain how someone already 'a determined enemy to every species of violence', as Wordsworth claimed to be as early as 1794, could also regard war against France as wholly unjustified by internal terror: 'we must not complain', she writes, 'that the genius of liberty ... should crush, with unrelenting step the pigmies of aristocracy or despotism which stood in its way' (1.3.239–40). Williams is not, of course, the only source for Wordsworth's conviction that Robespierre's career was a diversion, caused and goaded by Pitt's mistaken foreign policy, but she makes the case trenchantly. Depicting her work as an endless effusion of sensibility really does not do her justice.

One could of course argue that, ultimately, her aim is to justify the revolution, and to excuse its regrettable deviations, while Wordsworth's, ultimately, is to show how a youthful mind can be betrayed by its idealism into complicity with atrocious guilts. The problem is that the devil gets all the best tunes. The way I put it in 1989 was this:

> the three revolutionary books of the 1850 text of *The Prelude* present a spectacle of woe, an illustration of human ignorance and guilt. They constitute a confession that Wordsworth (like Coleridge, the poem's addressee, who is now recuperating in the Mediterranean) has been capable of being parted from his better self. But he has been taught to 'tame the pride of intellect'. Wordsworth presents himself as 'lured' into France (9: 34), over-confident in his capacity to understand the course of history, and (reversing Coleridge's use of the metaphor in France: an Ode), 'enchanted' by revolutionary illusions. Man, he comes to feel, is mocked by possession of the 'lordly attributes of will and choice', having in himself no guide to good and evil (11: 306–320).
>
> Yet no one who reads *The Prelude* attentively can fail to notice that Wordsworth's presentment of his earlier self has a candour which contrasts strikingly with Coleridge's lack of it in *Biographia Literaria*: it struck a Victorian reviewer [Macaulay]— who may not have noticed some of its subtle caveats—as 'to the last degree socialist, indeed Jacobinical'. Wordsworth is so bold to look on painful things that it becomes harder, the more familiar one becomes with the procedure of his account, to avoid the impression that while one of Wordsworth's consciousnesses is concerned to present himself as prey to delusions, another is anxious to present Coleridge with an image of one whose loyalty to the revolution—*well after the Great Terror of 1794, and by implication right up to the Coronation of Napoleon in 1804*—is, as a form of natural piety (loyalty of the self to the self), a matter of self-congratulation. *The Prelude* embodies within its critique of the ardour of undisciplined benevolence, a far more powerful critique of those who were not, at the time, capable of such 'indiscipline'. As one reads *The Prelude* it becomes very hard to escape the impression that as Wordsworth recollects, in tranquillity, the year of the terror, 'an emotion, kindred to that which was

before the subject of contemplation, is gradually produced and does itself actually exist in the mind' (I am of course quoting the 1800 Preface) so that the persona who address us from the midst of these events is a revolutionary persona, and if not a 'Terrorist', then certainly, in the phrase implausibly used of Coleridge by John Thelwall, a 'man of blood'.[1]

Williams twice refers to life in France as like living in a 'region of romance', and Wordsworth uses a similar phrase both of his own experience and of Beaupuy—it is hard to tell, in the latter case, whether Wordsworth is commending Beaupuy's chivalric nature or expressing a caveat about his grasp on reality. Many such images are designed to tell the truth twice: the truth of enthusiasm and the truth of disenchantment. In a moment of reprise he comments laconically, that 'I had approached, like other youths, the shield / Of human nature from the golden side' and this curious remark expects us to recall the mediaeval fable of knights in mortal combat over the true colour of a shield which was, in reality, silver on side and gold on the other. Williams, too, uses the term chivalry, in a manner that counters Burke's lament that the age of chivalry is dead: in the 1792 instalment of the *Letters* she reads the revolution as precisely a rebirth of chivalric feeling. Again, in her depiction of the British betrayals of the patriots of Naples, she comments that the Neapolitan patriots thought they could rely on Britain's 'laws, her manners, her customs, her remote and hereditary love of liberty, that proud pre-eminence, that lofty distinction above the other nations of the earth, which it is devoutly to be wished she may ever continue to deserve, and to secure' (*Sketches* 1: 198). Gary Kelly observes that this 'ironically echoes Burke's impassioned defence of "Antient chivalry" in *Reflections*.'[2] But if it does, one needs to be clear about the ground of the irony: both Williams and Wordsworth (the Wordsworth of the sonnets) associate a love of liberty (which is, in her phrase, both 'hereditary' and 'remote') with those republican moralists who in Wordsworth's sonnet:

---

1   '"Some other Being": Wordsworth in *The Prelude'*, *The French Revolution in Art and Literature: Yearbook of English Studies*, Volume 19 (1989) edited by J. R. Watson, 127–8.

2   *Women, Writing and Revolution 1790–1827* (Oxford: Clarendon Press, 1993), 195.

> ... knew how genuine glory was put on;
> Taught us how rightfully a nation shone
> In splendor: what strength was, that would not bend
> But in magnanimous meekness.

It is Milton, Wordsworth might be reminding the apostatic Burke, England hath need of, and it is Milton as the author of *The Tenure of Kings and Magistrates* whose mode of action embodied 'the heroic wealth of hall and bower'.

'Domestic carnage'

Williams's most vivid volumes depicted France in 1793–94, during which period Brissot and Gorsas were tried, as a time when 'men for the most part ignorant and unenlightened' were 'made arbiters of the liberty, property, and even lives of their fellow citizens' and yet insists—like Wordsworth praising 'humanity faithful to itself under worst trials'—that 'If France, during the unrelenting tyranny of Robespierre, exhibited unexampled crimes, it was also the scene of extraordinary virtue' (2.1.211). During the terror, she writes, licensing Wordsworth's slight tonal exaggerations, 'sometimes whole generations were swept away in at one moment' (216) and after those atrocities, she writes late in 1794, 'The past seems like one of those frightful dreams which presents to the disturbed spirit phantoms of undescribable horror, and "deeds without a name"; awakened from which, we hail with rapture the cheering beams of the morning' (257).

In Volume 2 of this second series, having briefly escaped the city to enjoy the consolations of Switzerland, Williams comments: 'I have no words to paint the strong feeling of reluctance with which I always returned from our walks to Paris, that den or carnage, that slaughter-house of man. How I envied the peasant his lonely hut! ... My disturbed imagination divided the communities of men into two classes, the oppressor and the oppressed; and peace seemed only to exist with solitude (2.2.4). Like Wordsworth, who also adopts the perspective that the Terror was an especially metropolitan virus, Williams resorts to *Macbeth* to express the horror of Paris: 'it cannot be called our mother but our grave ... where sighs and groans and shrieks that rend the air are made, not marked' (66). Under Robespierre, 'this high-priest of Moloch', her phrase, following his decree of 22nd Prairial that sentence could be passed without evidence or witnesses, 'multitudes were summoned at once... The husband was scarcely allowed time to bid his wife a last farewell, or the mother to recommend her orphan children to the compassion of such of the prisoners as might survive the general calamity' (98–99). Not surprisingly, like the younger poet whose revolutionary self saw silver as gold, and perpetually lamenting the vanished glory, 'For me the world has lost its illusive colouring' (100).

I might at this point dwell on Wordsworth's account of Paris in 1792 as coloured by Williams's wonderfully impressionistic pages on that city of fear, but I hasten on to glance at the central depiction of terror in Book 10. His brief account is derivative, powerful, and deeply ambivalent. In describing the terror, which began in June 1793, Wordsworth uses the oddest of his exculpatory tropes: the guillotine whirls like a child's windmill, with a kind of macabre innocence. One of Wordsworth's selves parenthetically questions the image, but does not censor it:

> Domestic carnage now filled the whole year
> With feast-days; old men from the chimney nook,
> The maiden from the bosom of her love,
> The mother from the cradle of her babe,
> The warrior from the field—all perished, all—
> Friends, enemies, of all parties, ages, ranks,
> Head after head, and never heads enough
> For those that bade them fall. They found their joy,
> They made it proudly, eager as a child,
> (If light desires of innocent little ones
> May with such heinous appetites be compared),
> Pleased in some open field to exercise
> A toy that mimics with revolving wings
> The motion of a windmill; though the air
> Do of itself blow fresh, and make the vanes
> Spin in his eyesight, that contents him not,
> But, with the plaything at arm's length, he sets

> His front against the blast, and runs amain,
> That it may whirl the faster. (1850, 10: 356–74)

The 'radical' edict which released the worst phase of the Terror (by permitting mass verdicts) was passed on June 10, 1793. Ten years later *The Prelude* certainly expresses in these lines a horror of violence, but Wordsworth seems equally capable of finding images expressive of something which is not merely horror, but a kind of dreadful fascination. Perhaps Wordsworth the philanthropist really was a 'determined enemy to every species of violence', as he told Matthews in June 1794, but, if so, he had not been so for very long.

A second 'childhood' image is introduced at 10: 391, dignified by its association with both Classical and English myth: 'The Herculean Commonwealth had put forth her arms and throttled with an infant godhead's might / The snakes about her cradle.' Part of its function is to prepare for the curious usage of the terms 'treachery' and 'desertion' in the nightmare passage which follows: Wordsworth presents himself as tortured 'through months, through years, long after the last beat/ Of those atrocities' (well into the Racedown period, that is) by nightmares of imprisonment, nightmares in which he appears to plead before unjust tribunals 'with a voice / Labouring, a brain confounded, and a sense, / Death-like, of treacherous desertion, felt / In the last place of refuge—my own soul'. The ambiguity is of the sharpest order: would it be more treacherous to plead for or against the 'accused'? Is he harbouring treacherous disloyalty to the infant commonwealth or (since the 'radicals', as some like to call them, dispensed with defence lawyers) to its victims? The function of the 'Herculean Commonwealth' image is to give weight to the less expected sense, that the treachery is to the infant commonwealth, the rough beast that born-again human nature turns out to be.

Such sympathies make it a little hard to see why Robespierre should come in for such rhetorical vengeance as he receives at Wordsworth's hands in 10.481–603. If those of the Poole circle in 1794 could view Robespierre as 'a ministering angel of mercy, sent to slay thousands that he might save millions'[1] why should Wordsworth react so differ-

---

1   Mrs Sandford, *Thomas Poole and his Friends* (2 vols, 1888), 1: 105.

ently, unless, perhaps, he is following the course of Williams's more tender sensibility? It may be that Wordsworth sees Robespierre as having given too many hostages to Tory propagandists and having—therefore—fuelled counter-revolutionary zeal. But there is a further consideration. Wordsworth, it seems to me, is less single-minded on the question of Robespierre than Helen Maria Williams, because, as the steely nature of his justification of regicide shows, his Jacobin *alter ego* was far closer than hers to the 'angel of mercy' so lightly spoken of in Nether Stowey, and which the poet of 1805 is relieved to lay to rest. Unlike hers, his account is tinged with guilt: Robespierre's death liberates both Wordsworth and Williams, but it does so in different ways.

'Come now, ye golden times'

I combine two of Williams's most joyful and comparatively untroubled passages, both from late 1794, when it appears that for her, as for Wordsworth, it was bliss to be alive and very heaven to be young:

> Surely it was glorious to be a leader of the revolution; for, although the sun of liberty, like the orb of day when seen through opposing mists, has been turned into blood, its dawning beams were radiant, and it will again shake off the foul vapours that have hung around it, and spread that unsullied light which exhilarates all nature (2:2.23).
>
> Upon the fall of Robespierre, the terrible spell which bound the land of France was broken; the shrieking whirlwinds, the black precipices, the bottomless gulphs, suddenly vanished; and reviving nature covered the wastes with flowers and the rocks with verdure (2.3.190).

In Wordsworth's account of this moment, the announcement by a passing traveller of Robespierre's death occasions from Wordsworth a 'hymn of triumph', and (in 1805) 'glee of spirit' and 'joy in vengeance'. It is presented as reawakening and reactivating Wordsworth's sense of himself as a power: his boyhood mastery of the horses of Furness usurps upon the fading echoes of the horsemen of apocalypse. The Wordsworth who with his boyhood associates 'beat with

thundering hoofs the level sand' now sees himself, 'an active partisan', helping to cleanse the Augean stables (another image employed
by Williams, in *Sketches*, 2: 21), tranquillise the 'madding factions',
and further 'the glorious renovation' of mankind. The shadow has
passed, and its passing is recorded in a dawn image: 'Come now, ye
golden times... as the morning comes / From out the bosom of the
night come ye'. It is now that he expects the republic to enjoy tri-
umphs which will be 'Great, universal, irresistible'.

Very sensibly, Wordsworth noted in the 1805 manuscript (MS.Z)
his intention to close Book 10 with that line and begin a new book (as
in the so-called 1850 version he does) with the optimistic statement
that 'From this time forth, in France, as is well known, / Authority
put on a milder face'. Authority's milder face sounds like personi-
fication, but we can in fact identify that face. It is the face of Jean-
Baptiste Louvet, the man Wordsworth has already credited with the
first denunciation of Robespierre. Louvet is now President of the
National Assembly, and one of Helen Maria Williams's circle. His
administration would soon prove to be another disappointment, but
for the moment the shadow has passed.

Wordsworth's model again seems to be Helen Maria Williams who
wrote of the same event, 'With what overwhelming sensations did I
receive the tidings of the fall of Robespierre (July 27th, 1794), which
was to change the colour of my life and give peace and consolation
to so many millions of my fellow creatures!' (*Memoirs* [1795], 85).
Her account of this restoration is given as an anticipation, while still
narrating the terror, and she cautions herself, 'But I must not thus
anticipate'. In neither account is the revolutionary dawn a once only
event—it happens at least once per volume, in Williams, in each of
France's succeeding mini-revolutions. Wordsworth is not quite so
prodigal with dawns, but *The Prelude* is so written as to instil serous
doubt about when Wordsworth felt that 'Bliss was it in that dawn to
be alive / But to be young was very Heaven' (10: 689 / 11: 105 ff).

The passage is too well known to quote at length. If the blissful
dawn occurred in the Summer of 1792, it is well nigh impossible to
see why, in the same passage, Wordsworth refers to himself as

> Not caring if the wind did now and then

> Blow keen upon an eminence that gave
> Prospect so large into futurity.

As a trope for one who knows of nothing worse than the fall of the Bastille—and the over-enthusiastic use of 'la lanterne'[1]—this is somewhat overblown.

All that prevents one from concluding that the 'blissful dawn' is biographically (as well as textually) experienced after rather than before the death of Robespierre is, of course, the *subsequent* remark (at 11: 173): 'In the main outline, such it might be said / Was my condition, till with open war / Britain opposed the liberties of France'. This, however, is a characteristically nebulous 'dating'. In June 1793, Wordsworth was watching the fleet assemble off the Isle of Wight, but the phrase 'open war' seems inapplicable to any military action before the naval engagements of late summer and October 1793, involving Admirals Howe and Hood—a full year after the September Massacres. The event which is specifically blamed for clouding the blissful dawn, is not, in the first place, the onset of Robespierre's terror but Pitt's military intervention. And we have yet to catch a glimpse of that Wordsworth for whom war and other reverses merely prompt him to adhere 'more firmly to old tenets', and whose goaded mind takes on the mantle of Robespierre, dragging 'all precepts, judgements, maxims, creeds, / Like culprits to the bar' (11: 295) and probing (in 1805) 'the living body of society/ Even to the heart' (*1805*, 10.875).

The Prelude was not, of course, Wordsworth's first attempt to depict such remorseless pursuit of self-elected values. The Character of Rivers, or Oswald, in Wordsworth's political drama *The Borderers*, explores it fully—and, it seems to me, may well originate less in the works of the amiable William Godwin, who is usually blamed for Oswald's fanaticism, than in Williams's wonderful description of the mountain, 'that elevated region, where, aloof from all the ordinary feelings of our nature, no one is diverted from his purpose by the weakness of humanity, or the compunction of remorse' (1.4.1).

Wordsworth's hymn of triumph at the passing of the shadow,

---

1   See Williams's comment on 'la lanterne', used by an over-ethusiastic populace as an impromptu gallows (*Letters* 1.1.80–81).

Robespierre, one may conclude, is only partly occasioned by what he felt about the death of Robespierre himself. A major element is relief, felt at the time of writing, at the dethroning of an unfeeling self whose depredations upon the living body of society and nature's holiest places are quite clearly presented as an internalisation of Robespierre's sanguinary practices. One feels the same deeply personal investment in the astonishing reference to the coronation of Napoleon in 1804.

> This last opprobrium when we see the dog
> Returning to his vomit; when the sun
> That rose in splendour, was alive, and moved
> In exultation among living clouds
> Hath put his function and his glory off,
> And turned into a gewgaw, a machine,
> Sets like an Opera phantom.

If this precise application of Old Testament metaphor (the dog returning to its vomit) has a parent, it is one Gilbert Wakefield, the mid-mannered Fellow of Jesus, who went to prison for two years for seditious libel, for having published (as Wordsworth did not) his own *Reply to the Bishop of Llandaff*. To Wakefield, the mere possibility of a restoration of monarchy in France is a case of the dog returning to its vomit—and how that metaphor found its way into *The Prelude* is a matter of conjecture (Wakefield does not figure in either volume of Duncan Wu's *Wordsworth's Reading*). If this image is a collective usage—passed, perhaps, from magazine to magazine or mouth to mouth—what of others? What of that sun turned into a gewgaw? Pitt's cabinet as 'base as vermin'? Robespierre as chief regent of the tribe of Moloch? The terrorists like a child with a windmill? The double-sided shield of human nature? This, if one believes in the primacy of paramount poetic genius, is tantamount to a domino theory of poetic agency—once one image is counterfeit, the currency is devalued. But then we know next to nothing of the *viva voce* transmission of perceptions.

The image may be borrowed, but his animus is real enough. And here I think one has to recognise a real difference from Williams: a violence of diction that betrays a significant trauma. In some respects, Wordsworth's investment in France was deeper than Williams's: she rode the September massacres and the execution of Louis, but she never condones the Jacobin terror of 93–94 to which something in Wordsworth was strangely drawn. We see that 'something' in the curious rhetoric of Book 10 where Wordsworth notes among the observers of the terror those who 'doubted not that providence had times of vengeful retribution' (10: 340), and suggests that some spirit fell on *him* that linked him with the ancient prophets who

> Wanted not consolations ...
> when they denounced
> On towns and cities, wallowing in the abyss
> Of their offences, punishment to come (10: 440)

Twenty years after his vision of human sacrifice on Salisbury Plain, sacrifice with which his imagination is strangely complicit, and ten years after he wrote it up in *The Prelude*, Wordsworth implied something not dissimilar concerning the consolations of Waterloo: *'Imagination—ne'er before content'* with the best that victory could do, *'stoops'* to this victory (my italics).[1] Did Helen Maria Williams, to whom Crabb Robinson sent a copy of the Waterloo volume, recognise the echo, and its subtle compliment? The phrase is (very nearly) her own. She, too, enjoyed a good battle: carnage did not repel her in principle, and a large part of the eight volumes of letters celebrates French victories—the same victories, by and large, that Wordsworth celebrated in the 1790s—just as they jointly rejoiced in Waterloo in 1814. She wrote of France's victories in the Pyrenees, in Holland and over the Austrians in Crevecoeur, Coblentz, etc, in 1793–94 that *'Imagination toils after victories like these'*. She attributed such victories, snatched from the jaws of defeat (the Austrians were 'almost within view of Paris' in 1793), to a people inspired by liberty—not to their commanders, or the convention, and least of all to 'the Mountain'. 'What then in four short months has driven these mighty

---

1   'Thanksgiving Ode', *The Poems of William Wordsworth: Collected Reading Texts from the Cornell Wordsworth*, ed. Jared Curtis (Humanities-Ebooks, 2009) 3: 87, lines 153–6..

hosts from the frontiers of the republic? What has armed not only the young but has renovated the vigour of the old? What but that holy flame which liberty kindles in every heart but that of the base and degenerate?' (*Letters*, 2.4.217).

Much the same perspective animates Wordsworth in writing of the Men of Killicrankie in 1803, of the heroes of Spain in 1807, and of Waterloo in 1815. The major difference between her response to Waterloo, in her 1816 *Narrative*, and his, is that she repeatedly eulogises Wellington—which Wordsworth markedly fails to do at any point. The grounds of her eulogy are that Wellington is both a more brilliant commander than Napoleon (she quotes one of his commanders to the same effect) *and* more magnanimous. She devotes a patriotic paragraph to how Wellington deployed his troops outside Paris and invited the French Generals to walk through his lines and inspect his forces and dispositions (brilliant defensive dispositions had been his forte since Vimeiro, his first victory in the Peninsular War), whereupon they sensibly declined the field—saving much unnecessary loss of blood. The same patriotism surfaces in another work of 1816. In her work *On the Late Persecution of Protestants in the South of France*, very much addressed to her loyal English audience, she writes one of what Gary Kelly calls one of her 'familiar apostrophes':

> Favoured and glorious England! How poor are the trophies of other nations compared with those which encircle her brows! She has ever the pre-eminence in all the counsels of philanthropy; the arbitress of moral action—the guardian of the wronged, whatever region they inhabit, with whatever colour they may be tinged. (56)

The Wordsworth of *The Excursion* is capable of similar pride in his nation, but such sentiments are a far cry from his 1803 *cri-de-coeur*:

> we have seen
> Fair seed-time, better harvest might have been
> But for thy trespasses; and, at this day,
> If for Greece, Egypt, India, Africa,
> Aught good were destined, Thou wouldst step between.
> England! all nations in this charge agree...

Judging on such sentiments alone one would be hard pressed to decide which of these writers was destined to become poet laureate, and which would become a permanent exile.

The pivot of disillusionment with France, for both poets, was of course Napoleon. Writing in 1827 Williams confesses her early adulation, saying how flattered she felt when Bonaparte addressed her on her morning ride in the Bois de Boulogne: 'My enthusiasm' she admits 'was totally fervent' (*Souvenirs* [1827], 132). But even her 1798 eulogies of Napoleon as 'invulnerable as Achilles and invincible and fortunate as Caesar' (*Sketches* 2: 158) can be matched by a figure like Sheridan who said of Napoleon's exploits 'never since the days of Hannibal have such splendid events opened on the world'. In April 1802, however, Bonaparte dissolved the Tribunate (to do away with the republicans who stood in his way); in May he reintroduced slavery; on 2 August 1802 he took the title of First Consul for life. In France, Lafayette, Williams and Kosciuszko gave up hope at this point—and at the same historical moment—Wordsworth's sonnets appear 'fourteener by fourteener' as E. P. Thompson once put it, to express the same revulsion. 'The rapid successive graduations to the consulate for life, and thence to the imperial purple' Williams says, 'dispelled all illusion, and displayed the undisguised truth.' She adopts Macbeth: 'Thou hast it now, King, Cawdor, Glamis, all...'. Wonderful![1]

I hope this chapter has already shown that there is more to their relationship than two sonnets and two evenings in Paris. If I were given to conclusions, I would like to adumbrate two. First, that there are not two but three co-authoring elements in the 1805 *Prelude*'s account of the revolution. In 1989 I identified two: a somewhat Robespierrean 'shadow' reanimated in the act of writing, and sympathising with the terrorists, who debates with what Wordsworth seems to see as his true but temporarily occluded self. I would now want to add a third 'self', taking part in a complex negotiation as the writing proceeds, namely an anima whose tears flow for the terrorized, and who

---

1   *Narrative of the Events Which Have Taken Place in France from the Landing of Napoleon Bonaparte on the 1st March, 1815, till the Restoration of Louis XVIII. 1815* (2nd edition, John Murray, 1816), 12.

is capable of ebullient faith and resilient jouissance. Another way of putting this would be to suggest that Wordsworth's poetic selfhood in *The Prelude* is quite capable of what Keats called 'negative capability', and is a lot harder to pin down that we tend to suppose. The same applies to that supposedly egotistical poem *The Excursion*, in which, compared with the stoical Wanderer, the despairing Solitary, and the self-confident Pastor, the figure who is the hardest to 'see' is in fact the Poet.

My second conclusion (by way of introducing the next chapter) is that one reason that Wordsworth's reflections on the blissful dawn can rise to such *animation*, always the work of the *anima*, is that his sensibility remains very much of the kind that in 1786, thrilled to Helen Maria Williams's imagined tears.

2. An Affair of Sensibility[1]

Twilight Tears

In 1786 a poetical schoolboy by the name of William Wordsworth, seems to have conceived a passionate admiration for an older woman. Not quite 17, he published—under a pseudonym—his first sonnet, *On Seeing Miss Helen Maria Williams weep at a tale of distress*. It is a fan-letter, and what it does, embarrassingly enough, is depict an adolescent swooning—becoming faint—at the very thought of a passionate tear on the cheek of his beloved Miss Williams. Her role in the poem ends with the second word. From then on until the *volta*, the sensation's are the boy's, whose ecstasy is narrated thus:

> She wept.—Life's purple tide began to flow
> In languid streams through every thrilling vein;
> Dim were my swimming eyes—my pulse beat slow,
> And my heart was swelled to dear delicious pain.
> Life left my loaded heart, and closing eye;
> A sigh recalled the wanderer to my breast;
> Dear was the pause of life, and dear the sigh
> That called the wanderer home, and home to rest.

Thus far the sonnet luxuriates in concocted sympathy with someone else's sympathy for we know not what, and the ratio of response to stimulus does raise the question whether this schoolboy might not be sending sensibility up. But at the *volta*, the poem makes an attempt to achieve some critical distance; or if that seems an overstatement, to at

---

1   This essay is much indebted to Deborah Kennedy's '"Storms of Sorrow': The Poetry of Helen Maria Williams', in *Man and Nature, Proceedings of the Canadian Society for Eighteenth-Century Studies*, Volume 10 (Edmonton 1991), 77–91; and to the same scholar's 'Hemans, Wordsworth and the "Literary Lady", *Victorian Poetry*, 35:3 (1997) 267–85.1997.

least encapsulate in the sestet a view of his idol's sensibility.

> That tear proclaims—in thee each virtue dwells,
> And bright will shine in misery's midnight hour;
> As the soft star of dewy evening tells
> What radiant fires were drowned by day's malignant power,
> That only wait the darkness of the night
> To cheer the wandering wretch with hospitable light.

Helen Maria Williams was then 25, and had just achieved some celebrity with her *Poems in Two Volumes* of 1786 (a title her young admirer will borrow twenty one years later with the sole distinction of a comma). She received a glowing review, spread over two issues of the *European Magazine*. To the same *European Magazine*—advised perhaps by his canny coach and schoolmaster William Taylor— Wordsworth sent his poem. The sonnet's over-indulgence makes it easy to disregard what I take to be Wordsworth's point: the literature of sensibility is indeed lachrymose, and in the case of some of its practitioners largely self-absorbed, but Williams is distinguished for having fairly consistently applied her sensibility to what might be termed protest poetry.

The term 'Sensibility', Janet Todd remarks, may indicate merely 'an innate sensitiveness or susceptibility revealing itself in a variety of spontaneous activities such as crying, swooning and kneeling', and thus be regarded as a condition or even derangement of the nervous system; but in literary history it has also 'come to denote the movement discerned in philosophy, politics and art, based on the belief in or hope of the natural goodness of humanity and manifested in a humanitarian concern for the unfortunate and helpless'.[1] Broadly defined, therefore, it can indicate both emotional susceptibility of an extreme and debilitating variety, as depicted in the octave of Wordsworth's sonnet, and a kinetic mode of empathy, of the kind Helen Maria Williams's poetry, at its best, and Wordsworth's own poetry in the 1790s aspire to.

In her narrative poems Williams applies emotion, specifically the experience of empathy, to the service of humane feeling, call-

---

1   *Sensibility: an Introduction*, Methuen 1986, 7.

ing attention to lives wasted in warfare, colonial conflicts, slavery or poverty. 'She wept' indeed, but she wept to a purpose. One might regard her, more than her contemporaries, as having begun the alliance between good writing and good causes that Charles Dickens eventually came to epitomise: as her mentor, the celebrated dissenter Andrew Kippis would have wished, she is as far as possible from 'art for art's sake'. And as Wordsworth observes in the last line of his sonnet, which itself marries the social to the sentimental, the purpose, the raison d'être, of those evening stars is 'To cheer the wandering wretch with hospitable light.'

We do not know which of several possible 'tales of distress' Wordsworth imagined his heroine weeping over; her two-volume collection (small pages, large print, generous margins and a quarter of it devoted to a list of subscribers!) contains several obvious candidates. One is *An American Tale*, in which the principal characters are on opposite sides of the American War, widely perceived at the time as a civil war because it divided so many in what was then called British North America: the heroine's father fights for the British, and her lover for the Americans (it isn't even made clear how she perceives her own nationality). She makes her way into the thick of battle to tend her dying father who is already being tended by her lover Edward, both males seeing the other primarily in terms of their humanity, not their uniform. The relevance to Wordsworth of her subject matter is perhaps almost too obvious to mention. As Wordsworth progressively develops his own voice in the giant strides that take him from *An Evening Walk*, to *The Female Vagrant* and *The Ruined Cottage,* it is in poems dealing with virtually the same topos. His first really affecting destitute, the war-widow of *An Evening Walk* (1793) loses her enlisted husband 'on Bunker's charnel hill' (254). The American War turns the press-ganged sailor of *Salisbury Plain* (1793–5) into a murderer, and its Female Vagrant into another war widow, and causes Margaret's husband in *The Ruined Cottage* (1796) to take the king's shilling. Wordsworth's purpose, like Williams's, is to invite readers to feel for passions not their own, in the context of sufferings caused by Britain's wars upon liberty.

The American War ended only two years before Williams's *Poems in Two Volumes*. The most grandiloquent poem in her collection, *An Ode on the Peace* celebrates the end of this war and contains stanzas suggestive of the Female Vagrant's terrible sufferings as a camp-follower:

> The object of her anxious fear
> Lies pale on earth, expiring, cold,
> Ere, winged by happy love, one year
> Too rapid in its course has roll'd:
> In vain the dying hand she grasps,
> Hangs on the quivering lip, and clasps
> The fainting form, that slowly sinks in death,
> To catch the parting glance, the fleeting breath.
> Pale as the livid corse her cheek,
> Her tresses torn, her glances wild,—
> How fearful was her frantic shriek!
> She wept—and then in horrors smil'd:
> She gazes now with wild affright,
> Lo bleeding phantoms rush in fight—
> Hark! on yon mangled form the mourner calls,
> Then on the earth a senseless weight she falls

Wordsworth's female vagrant—from whom he will develop the tragic figures of Margaret in *The Ruined Cottage* and Emily in *The White Doe of Rylstone*—presents herself as 'dog-like, wading at the heels of war', exposed to pestilence and to 'the shriek [a palpable echo of Williams's frantic shriek] that from the distant battle broke'. Her sufferings are equally phantasmagoric in places, and the wonderful closing alexandrine of *The Female Vagrant* offers an intenser variant on Williams's 'senseless weight': 'She wept because she had no more to say / Of that perpetual weight which on her spirit lay'.

The same theme, of humanity transcending difference, is writ large in Williams's six-Canto quasi-historical poem *Peru*—in a genre which Robert Southey would make his own—dealing with the Spanish massacre of the Incas during the native uprising against Pizarro in 1780. In each Canto of Williams's poem, a fiancée, a daughter, or a wife, attends the death of a figure whose sufferings are caused by the native rising against Pizarro in 1780, led by a figure not unlike Toussaint l'Ouverture, in this case Topa Amaru II.[1] *Peru* is not, like Southey's *Madoc*, based realistically on the detail of history. Its reduction of events to a succession of severed families engaged in mourning or rejoicing would be very tiresome if it were not in fact relatively short. But it does have one great merit. Unusually for poetical raptures of the late eighteenth century the language rarely obscures the feeling. The reviewer for the *European Magazine* commended her, above all her compeers, for 'elegant simplicity', for the 'easy flow of her versification' and for 'real genuine poetic simplicity'. In Canto 6, the tyrant Alphonso, who has in mind to enjoy the heroine Aciloë, has been torturing her father to gain her assent:

> At length she trembling cried, 'the conflict's o'er,
> *My heart, my breaking heart can bear no more—* [2]
> Yet spare his feeble age—my vows receive,
> And oh, in mercy bid my father live!'

Alphonso, however, is prevailed upon by the devout and kindly priest (the historical Las Casas) to let Aciloe unite instead with her lover Zamor. Listen to two things in this climactic scene. First the varied way in which the lines break (the usual sign of unpoetical poetry at this date is relentlessly predictable rhythms, as in most of the work of Hannah Laetitia Barbauld); second the relative naturalness of the phrasing (another sign of bad poetry is the frequency with which artificial phrasing leads one into reading errors, such as mistaking verbs for nouns or vice versa, so one has to keep re-reading sentences).

---

1   Chapter 6 of Frederick Burwick's *Romantic Drama: Action and Reaction* (Cambridge University Press, 2008) states that 'It was Cora's scene in Peru that prompted the young Wordsworth, who had neither met nor even seen Helen Maria Williams, to write his sonnet, "On Seeing Helen Maria Williams Weep".'. Burwick examines Williams's principle sources: William Robertson's *History of America* (1770) and Jean-François Marmontel's *Les Incas, ou la destruction de l'empire du Perou* (1777). As will be seen, I am less sure that it was necessarily Peru that prompted Wordsworth's sonnet.

2   Wordsworth echoes this line in *The Vale of Esthwaite* the following year: "Twas done. The scene of woe was o'er / My breaking soul could bear no more', though such lines are so common that he might just as well be echoing a virtually identical line in 'An American Tale' earlier in the Williams volume: 'My panting soul can bear no more'.

Alphonso's soul was moved—'No more', he cried,
'My hapless flame shall hearts like yours divide.
Live, tender spirit, soft Aciloë, live,
And all the wrongs of mad'ning rage forgive.
Go from this desolated region far,
These plains, where av'rice spreads the waste of war;
Go, where pure pleasures gild the peaceful scene
[...]'
In vain th'enraptured maid would now impart
The rising joy *that swells, that pains her heart*;
Las Casas' feet in floods of tears she steeps,
Looks on her sire and smiles, then turns, and weeps;
Then smiles again....

That characteristic phrase (in my italics), the joy 'that swells, that pains her heart' is of course echoed directly in the fourth line of Wordsworth's sonnet. If Williams is not entirely free of poetic diction and predictable rhymes (successive lines ending in 'lambent light', 'raptur'd sight', 'raging storm' and 'gentle form') one must remember that *An Evening Walk* is quite as redundantly adjectival and remorselessly crepuscular. Williams may also seem hackneyed in such formulae as 'Alagro swells the victor's captive train', but Coleridge uses precisely the same phrase in a climactic passage of *France: an Ode*.

So there is certainly a case for either *Peru* or *An American Tale* as the occasion of Helen Maria's imagined tears. But there is also third candidate, *Edwin and Eltruda, a Legendary Tale*. Williams launched her poetical career in 1782 with this over-long 'tale of distress', which is set in an ancient castle on the banks of the River Derwent. It may, for that very reason, have appealed to Wordsworth's imagination, and may even have impregnated it (to borrow his own metaphor) with numerous motifs destined to mature in later years. 'There is not much to be said for it', Jonathan Wordsworth sniffed in his Woodstock introduction to Williams. Well, maybe not, but it deals with a family conflict during the wars of the roses—a matter of great interest to the poet of *Brougham Castle*—and it shares with *The White Doe of Rylstone* the theme of a family riven by divided sympathies.

Wordsworth's *White Doe* is about protestant versus catholic sympathies during the Rising of the North, an ill-advised revolt against good Queen Bess. In Williams's simpler ballad, the heroine's father takes up his long forgotten lance in the cause of the Lancastrians, while her lover Edwin sides with York. Inevitably the lover wounds the father, recognizes what he has done, comforts him as he dies, then has to confess to Eltruda that he is her father's assassin.

It was not for its plot that Wordsworth is likely to have admired this poem. These blissful escapes from grief into eternity are not his terrain at all: his heroes and heroines have to do that much more difficult thing, they wrestle with what *The Borderers* called the 'after-vacancy' and endure their desolation without the solace of what Keats called 'easy death'. He is much more likely to have been struck by certain promising motifs, one of which is the Dorothean character of its heroine. Dorothy Wordsworth's tenderness over butterflies will be extolled in his own *Poems, in Two Volumes*. Here is Eltruda's.

> For the bruised insect on the waste,
> A sigh would heave her breast;
> And oft her careful hand replac'd
> The linnet's falling nest.

Eltruda also feels for those less fortunate than herself, and has the power to pour a Dorothean balm on neighbourly suffering…

> Full oft with eager step she flies
> To cheer the roofless cot,
> Where the lone widow breathes her sighs,
> And wails her desp'rate lot (1: 69–70)

She is, one might say, a sort of practical, caring Lucy figure:

> As drest in charms, the lonely flower
> Smiles in the desert vale;
> With beauty gilds the morning hour,
> And scents the evening gale;
>
> So liv'd in solitude, unseen,
> This lovely, peerless maid;

> So grace'd the wild sequestered scene,
> And blossom'd in the shade[;]

> *A violet by a mossy stone*
> *Half hidden from the eye;*
> *Fair as star when only one*
> *Is shining in the sky*

I tease, of course. Just over ten years separate Helen Maria's two limpid stanzas about a blossoming maid from Wordsworth's intensifying metaphors in 'She dwelt', conjuring a 'Lucy' figure who 'dwelt among th'untrodden ways'. But, notwithstanding the difference in intensity, would one notice the join if one grafted the two poems in this fashion? It is as if they shared a poetical blood-group, whatever the difference in power. One could, by the way, do much the same with *Peru* and *An Evening Walk*, whose verse form is likewise identical.

Helen Maria's Lucy figure is not doom'd to remain 'unknown' as well as 'unseen'. Young Edwin 'charms her gentle breast', wooing her with no more guile than 'honour, sense and truth' (67) thus setting up the conflict of sensations without a name when the two men Eltruda loves takes opposite sides in the civil conflict brought about 'When York, from Lancaster's proud sway, / The regal sceptre claimed'. The poem's focus is not on the battle, still less the politics, but upon the sensations of father and daughter, daughter and lover at parting. Indeed Williams uses a familiar Wordsworthian manoeuvre (he uses it most effectively in *The Idiot Boy*) to excuse herself from narrating 'moving accidents':

> The timid muse forbears to say
> What laurels Edward gain'd;
> How Albert long renown'd, that day
> His ancient fame maintained.

> The bard, who feels congenial fire,
> May sing of martial strife;
> And with heroic sounds, inspire
> The gen'rous scorn of life,

> But ill the theme would suit her reed,
> Who, wandering thro' the grove,
> Forgets the conq'ring hero's meed,
> And gives a tear to love.

The tell-tale 'tear' again. If the 'Sohrab and Rustum' theme was good enough for Matthew Arnold we may perhaps excuse it in Williams. And the death of Albert does show a very welcome gift for the understated:

> His languid eyes he meekly rais'd
> Which seem'd for ever clos'd ;
> On the pale youth with pity gaz'd,
> And then in death reposed

It is a nice touch, too, that the dying father has spare capacity to sympathise with Edwin's distress—that he could *afford* to suffer, as Wordsworth said of his Pedlar.

The catastrophe, in which Albert's death is followed by Eltruda's and almost immediately by Edwin's, sounds, in synopsis, highly unpromising. As Deborah Kennedy puts it 'she dies of grief and he soon follows her' ('"Storms of Sorrow"', 80). If it takes somewhat longer in the working out than in this summary, this is because, one might venture to say (in words from the *Lyrical Ballads* preface), it is 'the feeling that gives importance to the action and situation', rather than vice versa, and the feeling here is dwelt upon with some subtlety and with appropriate sharpness. The focus is upon Edwin's apprehension and upon Eltruda's unwitting irony

> Could not thy hand, my Edwin, thine,
> Have warded off the blow ?
> For, oh, he was not only mine,
> He was thy father too!

This line of simplicity in English poetry frequently refreshes itself, appearing in Coleridge's *Mariner*, for example ('The body of my brother's son / Stood by me, knee to knee; / The body and I pulled at one rope, / But he said nought to me) or in Thomas Hardy's touching echo: 'and he spake not to me'. Very few contemporaries managed it. Dorothy Wordsworth did. But the poetic norm of the day is much closer to Hannah More's doggerel: 'In yon distant cottage sitting. / Far away in London Town, / Once you might have seen me knitting / In my simple kersey gown'.

At this moment Edwin, who has not sat down since he left the battlefield, passes out. While Eltruda tries to reanimate him, the reader has space to wonder how, when he comes to, he will break the yet unsuspected news to his nurse and lover, and how she will react. The news does in fact consign Eltruda to death, yet not before she utters a very strange and deeply suggestive death-song on the theme of mourning:

> But come let us together rove,
> At the pale hour of night;
> When the moon wand'ring thro' the grove,
> Shall pour her faintest light...
>
> We'll gather from the rosy bower
> The fairest wreaths that bloom:
> We'll cull my love, each op'ning flower,
> To deck his hallowed tomb...
>
> We'll shun the face of glaring day,
> Eternal silence keep;
> Thro' the dark wood together stray,
> And only live to weep. (89–90)

The speech of Wordsworth's 'mad' mother, who in 1798 will imagine living in the woods 'for aye' alone with her babe, springs instantly to mind as writing entirely consonant with this. So perhaps should the sestet of his sonnet to Williams. After all, Eltruda's simple declaration 'We'll shun the face of glaring day' is echoed and elaborated in his tribute-paying line 'What radiant fires were drowned by day's malignant power'.

So, which of these 'tales of distress did Wordsworth have in mind? It is not perhaps the most burning question in Romantic studies, but although Wordsworth's poems borrow phrases from both *An American Tragedy* and *Peru* I rest my case for *Edwin and Eltruda*.

Williams's 1788 volume contained, also, this *Sonnet to Twilight* which Wordsworth borrowed from a year or so later, and commended to Alexander Dyce in April 1833, for a proposed new collection to be entitled *Specimens of English Sonnets*:

> Meek Twilight ! soften the declining day,
> And bring the hour my pensive spirit loves ;
> When, o'er the mountain slow descends the ray
> That gives to silence their deserted groves
> Ah, let the happy court the morning still,
> When, in her blooming loveliness array'd,
> She bids fresh beauty light the vale, or hill,
> And rapture warble in the vocal shade.
> Sweet is the odour of the morning's flower,
> And rich in melody her accents rise;
> Yet dearer to my soul the shadowy hour,
> At which her blossoms close, her music dies—
> For then, while languid nature droops her head,
> She wakes the tear 'tis luxury to shed.

Anyone who has ever dipped into Wordsworth's first published book will be reminded instantly of the 'soft glooms' and sympathetic twilights that the poet wrote of in *An Evening Walk* (1793):

> Now o'er the soothed accordant heart we feel
> A sympathetic twilight slowly steal,
> And ever as we fondly muse, we find
> The soft gloom deepening on the tranquil mind
>   …
> Yet still the tender, vacant gloom remains;
> Still the cold cheek its shuddering tear retains.

There is nothing quite like a little soothing melancholy amid congenial glooms, and as the revival of critical interest in the sonnet revival of the late eighteenth century has shown, sensibility and twilight go together in a hundred sonnets of the day, as well as in numerous of Wordsworth's early poetic fragments. But Williams's *Twilight* is likely to have appealed to Wordsworth on several grounds, one of which is its rhetorical structure: a beauty in a major key (morning) is compared with one in a minor key (twilight), and a preference expressed for the latter. One very characteristic Wordsworthian contrast poem, in *Poems, in Two Volumes*, works very similarly. 'Moods of My Own Mind, No 3'—'O Nightingale thou surely art / A Creature of a fiery heart'—first celebrates and then dismisses the impassioned song of the Nightingale in favour of the Stockdove's 'homely tale' and concludes 'That was the Song, the Song for me!' Such shared structural choices are one ground, perhaps, of their long (mostly one-sided) affair.

The bulk of Wordsworth's juvenile verse experiments are in fact evening elegies, of which this example is the most impressive fruit (entitled *Written in Very Early Youth*, and dated 1786 by Knight, it was certainly in draft at Cambridge, c. 1790–1, and was heavily revised before for publication in 1802):

> Calm is all nature as a resting wheel.
> The kine are couched upon the dewy grass;
> The horse alone, seen dimly as I pass,
> Is cropping audibly his later meal:
> Dark is the ground; a slumber seems to steal
> O'er vale, and mountain, and the starless sky.
> Now, in this blank of things, a harmony,
> Home-felt, and home-created, comes to heal
> That grief for which the senses still supply
> Fresh food; for only then, when memory
> Is hushed, am I at rest. My Friends! restrain
> Those busy cares that would allay my pain;
> Oh! leave me to myself, nor let me feel
> The officious touch that makes me droop again.

In this instance, the closing argument appears to pay tribute to Williams's *Sonnet to Hope*, at which I shall glance later, though the power of the sonnet up to that point lies in its apparent ease, the beautiful cadence of the first line somehow accentuating the mildly metaphysical shock it conveys; the accumulation of comforts of a somnolent kind from the outer scene; the awareness of that healing power that Arnold would regard as Wordsworth's truest gift; the subtle and uncontentious balancing of the 'home-felt, and home-created' and efficacious harmony that is found in the scene, with the 'busy cares' of officious friendship that fail in healing. Its note is tranquil, but not mawkish. Like Helen Maria Williams rather than Charlotte Smith it leaves one the sense that comfort is not refused, nor is misery sought. A curious passage in *An Evening Walk* does show Wordsworth toying (at twenty-three!) with the kind of self-nursed woes in which Charlotte Smith and the adolescent Lord Byron specialised:

> —The pomp is fled, and mute the wondrous strains,
> No wrack of all the pageant scene remains,
> So vanish those fair Shadows, human Joys,
> But Death alone their vain regret destroys.

But the note of that last line is quite discordant with the broadly sanative, if conventional, tendency of *An Evening Walk*—not to mention the concern with suffering humanity (the toiling quarrymen, the anguished mother with her famished babes) that runs through the poem. Twilight and grief, do certainly compose the terrain on which Wordsworth meets Charlotte Smith and Helen Maria Williams, but there is even in these early poems an emphasis upon the accordant, the sympathetic, and the interactive.

Some of Williams's motifs (including possibly, in Edwin's tearless grief, the germ of thoughts that lie 'too deep for tears'), lay dormant in Wordsworth for another ten or twenty years, but her oeuvre may well have encouraged the most remarkable feature of his juvenilia— a premature fascination with the feelings of those separated by death, and an anxiety (which expresses itself most strongly in his own *Poems, in Two Volumes*) to compose poems that will compose the reader rather as the Derwent composed his infant thoughts. Much of Wordsworth's early poetry takes the form of elegy. Having lost both parents he not unnaturally develops a premature fascination with the feelings of those separated by death, and his most impressive very early sonnet, more impressive than the sonnet to Williams that sits next to it in the Cornell edition of the early poems, purports to be the work of a widower: 'Sonnet written by Mr—— immediately after the death of his Wife'.

> Come Nature let us mourn our kindred doom,

> My sun like thine is dead—and o'er my Soul
> Despair's dark midnight spreads her raven gloom
> Yes she is gone—he call'd her to illume
> The realms where Heaven's immortal rivers flow...

This Heaven, we note, is strangely Virgilian; the afterworld seems in need of the very illumination Mr H—— has lost. But 'Despair's dark Midnight' might be taking us into realms of Gothic, or Sensibility or Classical Underworlds, with all of which voices the juvenile Wordsworth experiments, taking his Gothic cue, as much as his sensibility one, from Miss Williams.

One poem in Williams's volumes, *Part of an Irregular Fragment found in a Dark Passage of the Tower*, not only roused the reviewers to real enthusiasm but had an immediate effect on Wordsworth: it inspired the seventeen year old to his most Gothic performance in the ghoul-haunted *Vale of Esthwaite*. Williams's wonderfully strangulated climax in the *Irregular Fragment*—

> Why backward turns my frantic eye...
> Two sullen shades, half-seen, advance!
> And fix my view with dang'rous spells
> Again! their vengeful look—and now a speechless– ...

—cries out for completion and is undoubtedly the inspiration of Wordsworth's hauntings. His desperate cry at one point in *The Vale of Esthwaite* seems to articulate precisely what Williams leaves unspoken—threatened by druid-like spectres the youthful hero cries out 'why fix on me for sacrifice'. But as Duncan Wu notes, Williams's *Fragment* is a politically motivated piece of Gothic in the best tradition of that 18th century genre: 'a poem which portrays the English monarchy as a succession of homicidal maniacs'.[1]

In his mature work, as we all know, Wordsworth harrows the Gothic, turning incipiently Gothic figures such as the Discharged Soldier—whose earliest prototype appears in *The Vale of Esthwaite*— into archetypes of human endurance. When he eventually writes his only attempt at a romance, *The White Doe*, he spiritualizes the theme to such an extent as to make it far too demanding to be popu-

---

1   Duncan Wu, *Romantic Women Poets* (Blackwell, 1997), 228

lar. Nonetheless, Williams's *Irregular Fragment* clearly and closely inspires his first ambitious poem, and that poem in turn is something we could dwell on as the vital quarry from which his greatest poetry is mined. Without *The Vale of Esthwaite* we would not have Wordsworth's first meeting with the prototype of the discharged soldier

> ... from his trembling shadow broke
> Faint murmerings—sad and hollow moans
> As if the wind sighed through his bones

or his first improvisation of numerous 'tales of distress', involving empathy with what he calls 'the long winter of the poor':

> I trust the bard can never part
> With Pity, Autumn of the heart!
> She comes and o'er the soul we feel
> Soft tender tints of Sorrow steal;[.]

Nor would we have, most powerfully of all, the first draft of the Prelude spot of time on the death of his father—

> Long, long upon yon naked rock
> Alone, I bore the bitter shock;
> Long, long, my swimming eyes did roam
> For little horse to bear me home,
> To bear me—what avails my tear?
> To sorrow o'er a father's bier

—or the self-diagnostic conclusion of that *Vale of Esthwaite* passage, deeply characteristic of the introspective vein in Wordsworth's mature poetry, 'I mourn because I mourned no more'.

Without Helen Maria Williams, in other words, we might never have had that *ur-Prelude*—and if we hadn't had the *ur-Prelude*, it is reasonable to wonder whether we would have had *The Prelude* itself. It is in these Williams-inspired juvenilia, after all, rather than in the friendship with Coleridge, that the one achieved and wholly satisfactory instalment of *The Recluse*—*The Prelude* of 1805—takes its origin. *The Prelude* is grown from tissues of *The Vale of Esthwaite*, and *The Vale* is inspired directly by Williams's poem of spectral encounter.

Certainly, without Williams, as shown in my first chapter, *The Prelude* might not have had its middle books. Because the Williams story does not end there, and it is not as poet who never quite realized her potential, that she lends him most aid, but as a very major writer of historical prose. In that department she stood head and shoulders above any rival poet of the day, and this is a matter I need to revisit— though with as little repetition as I can manage.

Affective elements in *The Prelude*

I have already dwelt on the evidence for suggesting that the account of the revolution we are all familiar with, in the *Letter to the Bishop of Llandaff* and in *The Prelude*, is both in general outline, in its politics, and in most of its particulars indebted to Helen Maria Williams's— indebted, I would still claim, to the point of plagiarism. Nor is this surprising: Williams realized the consistency that Wordsworth claims for himself in *The Prelude*. She is, in effect, the model for the 'I' of that poem, which is why one can tell his story in her words with a remarkable degree of precision. But in chapter one I emphasised the political content of their shared vision; in this chapter there are one or two more points to be made about the manner in which each poet tells the story of the revolution.

Perhaps the most striking stylistic, or strategic resemblance in their accounts, is the way in which both authors assume the stance of novitiates. Both Williams and Wordsworth need to have the significant sights and sites pointed out to them, and find it easier to grasp the real meaning and effect of the revolution through affecting human instances. Lured (9: 34) into a 'theatre, whose stage was filled / And busy with an action far advanced' (9: 94) Wordsworth described himself as 'unprepared with needful knowledge', until his tutorials with Michel Beaupuy. Unsurprisingly, for a poet, it takes the powerfully felt image of a hungry girl tied to a heifer, whose plight sums up for Beaupuy all that 'we are fighting for', to release in Wordsworth the closest thing he ever writes to a manifesto. His political science, before Beaupuy, amounted to a feeling that 'the best ruled not, and feeling that they ought to rule', a position rooted in his schooltime experience of 'ancient homeliness' in lakeland's admittedly untypical 'nook'. Now it extends to matters of representation, constitutionally defined. Williams, too, professes little skill in political science, except that as she disarmingly puts it in her first volume (rather like a real-life Esther Summerson): 'when a proposition is addressed to my heart I have some quickness of perception' (1.1.195). Indeed she summarises her political philosophy in her famous remark on the story of the du Fossé family: 'that system of politics must be best, by which those I love are made happy'.

The climactic story in her first volume—and her early volumes do tend to proceed from anecdote to anecdote—tells the story of this family, whom she met in England when they were refugees. The story exhibits the injustice of the *ancien régime*, in which a father uses the infamous *lettres du cachet* to imprison his son and prevent him from marrying a woman of lower rank. It is a characteristic enlightenment manoeuvre to allegorise an oppressive political system as a dysfunctional family and to equate bad kings (George III *vis-à-vis* America and Louis *vis-à-vis* France) with tyrannical fathers. At the close of the 9th Book of *The Prelude* Wordsworth famously rewrites this episode from Williams as the story of Vaudracour and Julia (Vaudracour meaning Woodcourt—an unusual Dickensian manoeuvre for him), which itself partially unveils his own French romance, his affair with Annette Vallon. More precisely, though, he emphasizes a subplot of Williams's story. In the next cell to du Fossé, in Williams's account, was a boy of fifteen who was

> incarcerated by his mother … confined for ten years and only released when all the prisons were thrown open by order of the National Assembly. But for this unhappy young man their mercy came too late.—his reason was gone for ever! and he was led out of his prison, at the age of five and twenty, a maniac (1.1.211).

Wordsworth's Vaudracour (another alter ego) ends up as a nervous wreck: 'His days he wasted—an imbecile mind'. So 'Vaudracour and Julia', as Wordsworth tells it, is given his characteristic doubleness—it is both an indictment of the ancien régime, and an oblique instance

of illegitimacy and untethered mind. And why 'Julia' one may ask?
Well it may, or may not, be significant that *Julia* just happens to be the
title of Williams's first novel, another critique of the ancien regime,
set in the Romantic north of England, and dealing with the later history of the Cliffords.[1]

An equally 'affective' moment in Wordsworth's account, this time
unfictionalized, relates to the fall of Robespierre, which I treated
briefly in chapter 1 but must now revisit but with a shift of emphasis. According to *The Prelude*, Wordsworth received the news while
crossing the Leven sands—

> O Friend! few happier moments have been mine
> Through my whole life than that when first I heard
> That this foul Tribe of Moloch was o'erthrown,
> And their chief Regent levelled with the dust

—and he comments, that this day deserves 'a separate chronicle'.

That chronicle is very odd, even by Wordsworth's standard of cir-
cumlocution. It begins with a description of the glorious mountains
seen across the Leven Sands—the mountains perceived like a 'glory'
over the pastoral vales 'among whose happy fields I had grown up'.
It digresses into a visit to the grave of William Taylor, at whose com-
mand he wrote his first poems—among them, of course, the sonnet
to Williams. Then it recalls itself to the precise scene on the day he
receives the news of the death of Robespierre, noticing how the scat-
tered travellers made their way 'In loose procession through the shal-
low stream / Of inland waters'; while the ominous sea 'Heaved at
safe distance, far retired'. At which point someone cries, without any
salutation, 'Robespierre is dead!' The news releases an extraordinary
'Hymn of Triumph', based on a passage from Williams which I have
cited on page 33:

> 'Come now, ye golden times,'
> Said I forth-pouring on those open sands
> A hymn of triumph: 'as the morning comes

---

1   The text of *The Prelude* (1805, 9: 549) appears to attribute this story to Beaupuy;
     its real source is acknowledged in *The Fenwick Notes* (55) as being 'a French
     lady', which Helen Maria Williams then was, having taken citizenship in 1817.

From out the bosom of the night, come ye...'

In fact, however, Book 10 concludes not with anticipation of constitutional renewal, though it does dwell on that prospect for some lines, but with a wonderful passage of regression:

> Thus interrupted by uneasy bursts
> Of exultation, I pursued my way
> Along that very shore which I had skimmed
> In former days, when—spurring from the Vale
> Of Nightshade, and St. Mary's mouldering fane,
> And the stone abbot, after circuit made
> In wantonness of heart, a joyous band
> Of school-boys hastening to their distant home
> Along the margin of the moonlight sea –
> We beat with thundering hoofs the level sand.

There is always something magical about a perfectly regular iambic pentameter levitating on its five pulsating stresses (this rarely happens because, in reality, most iambic pentameters make do with four). This one is especially magical because the horizontal line—conjuring those 'levels'—is also an artesian well, to use Seamus Heaney's metaphor, sinking a shaft back into childhood. The echo comes from Book 2, to the wonderfully convoluted narrative of a day at Furness Abbey—a day of boisterous activity enclosing a pearl of contemplation as he listens to a wren in the ruined nave of Furness Abbey in childhood's eternal summer. In other words, the day he recalls from childhood is an innocent version of the same blend of barely compatible sensations—calm and joy, exultation and vengeance, guilt and disturbance—that this moment of history involves. And to draw out one point of that comparison, Wordsworth's version of history—his sense of what the Fall of Robespierre means is not merely the same in substance as Helen Maria's. It is, like hers—like all of her major moments—a record of sensibility, or of how the moment felt.

A language for the sense of aftermath

The meeting Wordsworth had hoped for in the heady days of 1792, did not take place until 1820, by which time Robespierre and Napoleon were history, and both poets could meet on the grounds of mutual satisfaction in the outcome of Waterloo. For a man who had spent almost two decades being reviled by adulators of Napoleon—Hazlitt and suchlike—there must have been immense consolation in finding that his views of Napoleon, of Waterloo, and of Britain's role in Europe were broadly shared by the one person who most personified and most exemplified political consistency, and who, in identifying herself with the French cause had taken the road he did not take. Be that as it may, in Paris with Dorothy in 1820, Wordsworth made one of the most romantic gestures of his life. On the first of two evenings they spent with Helen Maria Williams—discussing one supposes both France and poetry—Wordsworth recited from memory this sonnet *To Hope* first published in her 1790 novel, *Julia*, and read by him—one supposes—at around that date.

> O, ever skilled to wear the form we love!
> To bid the shapes of fear and grief depart;
> Come gentle Hope! With one gay smile remove
> The lasting sadness of an aching heart.
> The voice, benign Enchantress! let me hear;

(Some poets reading the words 'thy voice benign enchantress' to Paris's most enchanting hostess might do so very seductively; perhaps he did?).

> Say that for me some pleasures yet shall bloom,—
> That Fancy's radiance, Friendship's precious tear,
> Shall soften, or shall chase, misfortune's gloom.
> But come not glowing in the dazzling ray,
> Which once with dear illusions charm'd my eye,—
> O! strew no more, sweet flatterer! On my way
> The flowers I fondly thought too bright to die;
> Visions less fair will soothe my pensive breast,
> That asks not happiness, but longs for rest!

It is likely that these soirées with William and Dorothy prompted Helen Maria to collect her later poetry for her *Poems on Various*

Subjects (1823).[1] When she did so she appended a footnote: 'I commence the Sonnets with that to Hope, from a predilection in its favour, for which I have a proud reason; it is that of Mr Wordsworth who lately honoured me with his visits while at Paris, having repeated it to me from memory, after a lapse of many years.'[2] He wasn't just flattering Williams: ten years later he commended the same sonnet to Alexander Dyce for his book of English sonnets, along with *To Twilight*. If a man—even a poet much given to composing poetry in memory before he wrote it down—remembers a poem, word for word, over a period of thirty years, one may suppose that he has some investment in its argument. So what appealed to him about this one?

One needs I think to dwell on the tropes in the sestet and to think of Wordsworth as having become, well before this meeting, pre-eminently the poet of endurance, of coming to terms with mortality—and having, I think, seen himself in those terms almost from the start. The 'Lucy poems'—whatever else they may have to do with—are primarily meditations on the fragility of life, and the need to absorb an acceptance of death into life's texture. And the elegiac lyrics of Wordsworth's *Poems, in Two Volumes* are, like the close of *Paul and Virginia*, shadowed by shipwreck. In the *Piel Castle* stanzas Wordsworth commends Beaumont for depicting 'That hulk which labours in the deadly swell', faces the 'trampling waves', and welcomes 'frequent sights of what is to be borne'. In its companion poem the *Ode to Duty* he trades illusory hopes for 'a repose that ever is the same' and in the great 'Ode' to which both of these are the preambles he consoles himself that 'in our embers is something that doth live'. Williams was only 28 when she wrote that sonnet to Hope, and Wordsworth a little over 34 when he wrote *Piel Castle*. But they are

---

1   Another outcome was that Dorothy acquired from Henry Crabb Robinson a copy of Williams's latest political publication, her 1819 *Letters on Events in France ... Since the Restoration*.

2   Actually Wordsworth had been re-reading Williams in 1817–1820. F. W. Todd, whose brilliant appendix in *Politics and the Poet: a Study of Wordsworth* (London: Methuen, 1957, pp 217–228) offers the first treatment of Wordsworth's debts to Williams, including the tale of Vaudracour and Julia, notes that Wordsworth's 'The Lament of Mary Queen of Scots' (composed 1817, first published in 1820) is 'little more than a recasting of "Queen Mary's Lament"', in Williams's 1786 *Poems in Two Volumes*.

both, already, poets of aftermath—of 'something that doth live'.

At 33 Williams was languishing in one of Robespierre's prisons adding sonnets to her translation of Bernardin de Saint Pierre's *Paul et Virginie*, whose heroine, by the way, dies by shipwreck, contending as did Captain John Wordsworth, with 'remorseless billows'. As with *Letters from France*, especially the volumes describing the Terror, and *Julia*, Wordsworth seems to have bought *Paul and Virginia* the year it came out, in 1795. This little novella of French enlightenment sensibility takes for its theme a story rather like Vaudracour and Julia or its source de in the du Fossé's tale, the cruel exercise of power in forbidding young love. A malicious aunt delays her niece's voyage home to her first love, until the stormy season, in the express hope that she will die. Summarised thus, it sounds remarkably like a parable of revolutionary hopes ('it is against that / That we are fighting') and one can also summarise its narrative structure in such a way as to make it redolent of *The Ruined Cottage*. It is, after all, told by a wise old man to a young stranger who wishes to know the sad history appertaining to an abandoned spot, once home to 'a few obscure individuals' (*Paul and Virginia*, 4–5).

What Wordsworth does with his material, however, is incomparably deeper than Saint Pierre can manage. One has only to compare Wordsworth's extraordinary struggle to conclude the poem with the bland close of *Paul and Virginia* to see the difference. Yet in the closing paragraphs one can see just as likely a source for the strategy and the cottage topos of *The Ruined Cottage* as the oft-cited lines from Southey's *Joan of Arc* are for its topos of the heart-sick mother:[1]

> 'Beloved family! ... those fountains which flowed for you, those hillocks upon which you reposed, still deplore your loss! No one has since presumed to cultivate that desolated ground, or repair those fallen huts. Your goats are become wild, your orchards are destroyed, your birds are fled, and nothing is heard but the cry of the sparrow hawk, who skims

---

1   Southey wrote: 'At her cottage door / The wretched one shall sit, and with dim eye / Gaze o'er the plain, where on his parting steps, / Her last look hung. Nor ever shall she know / Her husband dead, but tortured with vain hope / Gaze on—then heartsick turn to her poor babe / And weep it fatherless!' as printed by Coleridge in *The Watchman*, 1 March 1796 (CC2: 45).

around the valley of rocks. As for myself, since I behold you no more, I am like a father bereft of his children, like a traveller who wanders over the earth, desolate and alone.' ...

In saying these words, the good old man retired, shedding tears, and mine had often flowed, during this melancholy narration. (*Paul and Virginia*, 114)

To pass to these sentences from the closing passages of *The Ruined Cottage*, which dwell precisely on the rightness or wrongness of tears, on how to 'read the forms of things with a worthy eye', would be a very good example of bathos, or the art of sinking.

But the sonnets dispersed throughout the novel are (as they were in *Julia*) a different matter. Just as the haunting lyrics of Tennyson's *The Princess* crystallise Princess Ida's emotions, the sonnets are written supposedly to express the feelings of the exiled mother Madame de la Tour. They are poems of exile, both from homeland and from childhood. If one thinks back to the poems of 1802 in which Wordsworth selects butterflies glow-worms and suchlike as 'historians of my infancy' (not to mention the second of the 'Evening Sonnets' which associates childhood with 'sauntering' to 'pluck' wild strawberries (*EPF* 680–1)) it is easy to understand how Williams's *Sonnet to the Strawberry* might have appealed to him:

> The strawberry blooms upon its lowly bed:
> Plant of my native soil!

Other plants may deal in more potent fragrances, but for the speaker this plant calls up

> The vanish'd hours of life's enchanting spring;
> Short calendar of joys forever fled!

There is a 'Wordsworthian' implication that such memories have more power than those of later years precisely because they are early and more native to the soul:

> Thou bidst the scenes of childhood rise to view,
> The wild wood path which fancy loves to trace,
> Where, veil'd in leaves, thy fruit of rosy hue,

> Lurk'd on its pliant stem with modest grace.
> But, ah! when thought would later years renew,
> Alas! successive sorrows crowd the space.

A careless reading might suppose that the final lines here nullify the virtue of the strawberry plant, overtaken by sorrows; but in fact of course the logic is just the opposite. Such curative associations from early childhood retain their renovative or fructifying power, whereas our later years add little to the store of memory but 'successive sorrows'. The poem hints at the Wordsworthian thought that diversity of strengths attend us if but once we have been strong. In the sestet of *Sonnet to the Curlew*, there is more than a hint that life is woven of both joy and sorrow, beauty and fear, and in this sonnet we once again enter *Piel Castle* territory, with its trampling (Wordsworth) or troubled (Williams) waves:

> I love the ocean's broad expanse, when dress'd
> In limpid clearness, or when tempests blow.
> When the smooth currents on its placid breast
> Flow calm, as my past moments us'd to flow;
> Or when its troubled waves refuse to rest,
> And seem the symbol of my present woe.

Williams's sensibility, I have been suggesting, appealed to Wordsworth first as a melancholy youth making his first poetical experiments in Esthwaite, addressing endless elegies to bereft lovers and aged widowers. There is a limpid quality to her style that certainly appealed to him more than the extravagance of her contemporaries and helped to inspire the 'daring humbleness of language' that Coleridge so deplored in his ballad experiments. But her greatest gift to Wordsworth was undoubtedly the argument, the perspective, and many of the diagnostic tropes, of Books 9, 10 and 11 of *The Prelude*, of which, I have no doubt, she ought to be recognized as the most significant co-author. She, more than anyone else, lived the life that he imagines in that poem as the road he did not take. She bears the same relation to him, one might say, as that schoolboy who blew mimic hootings to the owls that they might answer him, and who died on the banks of Esthwaite; she is another vicarious self.

So how can one gauge the importance of Williams to Wordsworth? We all know of the paramount importance of Milton and Coleridge as poetic and intellectual influences on the middle and later Wordsworth. And it would be wrong to deny that such poets as Gray, Beattie, and Thompson and Cowper helped to mould his early style, especially where it is most florid. But I would suggest that there are three great influences on his early Gothic and elegiac poetry (there is very little in the early work that isn't in one of those two modes): Virgil, for his underworld obsessions; Spenser as a model of allegorical narration; and Williams, for the poetry of human suffering. Spenser is most obviously present in the stanza of *The Female Vagrant*, though he reappears in the romance of *The White Doe*. Virgil—now the Virgil of the *Georgics*—has the greater bearing on his pastorals, and Williams on his ballad verse, both in their 'daring humbleness of language' and their sensibility. Virgil, Spenser, Williams: I would not place her primus inter pares; but I would insist on her inclusion. Without these three, Wordsworth might have written as woodenly as Crabbe, or as preciously as Charlotte Smith.

Wordsworth and the Sensibility Sonnet

Peter Spratley has rightly called attention to the fact that modern criticism and modern editions have improperly severed the twenty 'Miscellaneous Sonnets' from the twenty-six 'Sonnets Dedicated to Liberty' in Wordsworth's design of the *Poems, in Two Volumes*. He complains, too, that we compound this offence by tending to read one or two of the former (such as Westminster Bridge and the Calais sonnet to Caroline) almost as honorary political sonnets, consigning the remainder to undeserved oblivion.[1] I would add that we have also,

---

1   Peter Spratley, 'Wordsworth's Sensibility inheritance: the Evening Sonnets and the 'Miscellaneous Sonnets'', *European Romantic Review*, 20:1 (January 2009) 95–115, p 112. For important work on Wordsworth and sensibility son-neteering, see Stuart Curran, *Poetic Form and British Romanticism* (Oxford University Press, 1986); Duncan Wu, 'Navigated by Magic: Wordsworth's Cambridge Sonnets', *Review of English Studies* 46 (1995) 352–65; Daniel Robinson, 'Reviving the Sonnet: Women Romantic Poets and he Sonnet Claim', *European Romantic Review*, 6 (1995) 98–127, and, also by Robinson, '"Still Glides the Stream": Form and Function in Wordsworth's *River Duddon* Sonnets', *ERR* 13 (2002) 449–64.

just as damagingly, severed both the political sonnets and the grander miscellaneous sonnets, and the tragic elegies that lead into the ode, from the wonderful outpouring of pansies, or pensées, in playful lyric form that are, or present themselves as being, no more than artless effusions of the moment, especially that most unWordsworthian of moments—the present. But I will return to that in chapter three.

Admittedly, Wordsworth's own claim to have been provoked into writing sonnets merely by reading Milton (or rather, having Milton read to him by Dorothy, possibly in tones that lessened the distinction between the Miltonic and the Sensibility sonnet)[1] licenses this critical erasure of the ample evidence that his 'Miscellaneous Sonnets' derive as much from the prolific sonneteering of the Age of Sensibility, and of course from those of Petrarch, as they do from the Miltonic. So, perhaps, does his decision not to mention one poet of sensibility in his list of masters from Shakespeare and Petrarch to Spenser and Milton in his much later sonnet 'Scorn not the Sonnet'. Then again, that later sonnet doesn't mention Sidney, either, and the critical reception of *Poems, in Two Volumes* may have decided him not to court more charges of effeminacy by mentioning Williams, Seward or Smith. Perhaps, when speaking to Miss Fenwick of his Miltonic conversion to sonnetry, he simply forgot that he had published 'Calm is all nature as a resting wheel' three months before the alleged Damascus moment of May 1802, and that this was one of a series of four 'evening sonnets' closely allied in theme and diction to *An Evening Walk* (1789).

Wordsworth clearly read Helen Maria Williams's *Poems* in 1787, as he read Bowles's *Fourteen Sonnets* in 1789, and Williams's *Julia* and Charlotte Smith's *Elegiac Sonnets* in 1790/91. He drew upon all three, and indeed continued reading Charlotte Smith for some months after Milton supposedly descended on him and showed him what else the sonnet could do. Of course, such lines as 'Calm is all nature as a resting wheel', and 'And all that might heart is lying still', and 'This sea that bares her bosom to the moon', and 'It is a beauteous evening, calm and free', and 'Still glides the stream, and shall for ever glide' have a tone (Lucy Aikin would have called it 'manly') that

---

1   Pamela Woof, ed., *The Grasmere and Alfoxden Journals*, 2002, 134–5.

owes nothing to such poets as Bowles or Smith—poets who practice the kind of poem that inspired Coleridge to define the sonnet as 'a small poem in which some lonely feeling is developed'.[1] Such lines take the sonnet into altogether different territory, and the power of the sonnets arises not from single lines merely but in the way the rhythms run majestically from line to line, as in this invocation of the sea:

> Listen! The mighty Being is awake
> And doth with his eternal motion make
> A sounds like thunder – everlastingly.

This particular voice owes nothing whatever to Milton, either. What we have in the Miscellaneous Sonnets, and occasionally in the *River Duddon* series,[2] is a voice that shows what the so-called 'prospect sonnet'—the conventional vehicle of sensibility sonneteers—can do when its author keeps his eye steadily fixed on his object, and his object (as in *Lyrical Ballads*, and as in *The Prelude*) is to show what kind of thinking emerges when the landscape in the poem is not merely a scenic backdrop, or, as in Smith, a carefully selected mirror of the melancholy soul, but is a partner in the thinking.

In giving Williams priority, over Smith, as a poet seriously congenial to Wordsworth, I am well aware that I champion the less prolific and indeed less accomplished poet. To prove a negative is of course impossible, so I will simply compare what Smith does in one sonnet, with what Williams does in another, and indicate why I think his own poetical practice is closer to that of Williams. This is Smith's *Sonnet to Night*, which Wordsworth 'particularly recommended' to Dyce:

---

1 *Sonnets from Various Authors*, 1796.
2 Mary Anne Myers, in a paper at the Wordsworth Summer Conference, 2009, argued persuasively that the River Duddon series is fundamentally Petrarchan. Petrarch, rather than Shakespeare, provides the basis for the Miltonic sonnet, and what Wordsworth admires in Milton's adaptation of the Petrarchan form is its greater unity. Rather than consisting of two or three 'movable parts' a sonnet should ideally suggest 'the image of an orbicular body,—a sphere—or a dewdrop' (LY 2: 653). Petrarch's importance to Wordsworth—it comes out very early in the form of his Esthwaite 'Sonnet written by Mr H——' (1787), in the closing paragraph of *Concerning the Convention of Cintra* (1809), in the *River Duddon* sonnets (1820), and in the *Fenwick Notes* (1843) where he celebrates this 'ardent and sincere patriot'—has long been underestimated.

I love thee, mournful, sober-suited night!
When the faint moon, yet lingering in her wane,
And veil'd in clouds with pale uncertain light
Hangs o'er the waters of the restless main.
In deep depression sunk, the enfeebled mind
Will to the deaf, cold elements, complain,
And tell the embosom'd grief, however vain,
To sullen surges and the viewless wind.
Tho' no repose on thy dark breast I find,
I still enjoy thee—cheerless as thou art;
For in thy quiet gloom, the exhausted heart
Is calm, tho' wretched; hopeless yet resigned.
While to the winds and waves its sorrows given,
May reach—tho' lost on earth—the ear of Heaven!

As a celebration of lassitude this is commendable, but what it celebrates is a condition that is, in all Wordsworth's treatment of heroines, from the Female Vagrant to Emily in *The White Doe*, and indeed in the Solitary of *The Excursion*, portrayed as undesirable. Its lines are heavily end-stopped and the quatrains self-enclosed. The poem is done with earthly life by line twelve, with its spiritless 'calm, tho' wretched; hopeless yet resigned' where the structure seems to imply a tension or contrast that is not there: the four terms are barely distinguishable, enacting an absence of options. In the couplet (and the usual defence of concluding couplets is that they can energise a close) the syntax is so turned on itself that it may take some effort to perceive that the subject of the verb 'reach' is 'sorrows'.

Here by contrast is Williams's *Curlew*:

Sooth'd by the murmurs on the sea-beat shore,
His dun grey plumage floating to the gale,
The curlew blends his melancholy wail
With those hoarse sounds the rushing waters pour.
Like thee, congenial bird: my steps explore
The bleak lone sea beach or the rocky dale,
And shun the orange bower, the myrtle vale,
Whose gay luxuriance suits my soul no more.
I love the oceans's broad expanse, when dress'd

In limpid clearness, or when tempests blow.
When the smooth currents on its placid breast
Flow calm, as my past moments us'd to flow;
Or when its troubled waves refuse to rest,
And seem the symbol of my present woe.

Despite the contiguity of the matter, the setting and some of the terms (Smith's mournful and Williams's melancholy most obviously) the contrast is immediate. Wordsworthianly, this speaker is called forth by the curlew, or like the curlew, to explore 'The bleak lone sea-beach or the rocky dale' shunning only the unwelcome 'gay luxuriance' of the orange bower. Where Smith's speaker loves sober-suited night because it is almost monotone, and the sonnet is so constructed as to enact its spiritual enervation in defiance of the energies in the scene itself (another Smith sonnet pleads with her native hills to 'teach a breaking heart to throb no more' [*Poems* 16: 8]), Williams, in her subtly integrated sestet, is drawn to the possibilities of difference, recognising gratefully the symbology of a peaceful past, and challenged equally by the tempestuous waves which are noted in the final phrase as seeming 'the symbol of my present woe', both of which terms admit the possibility of other outcomes. Lamb may have mentally included Williams in his understandable diatribe in 1798 against 'the race of sonnet writers & complainers, Bowless and Charlotte Smiths, & all that tribe, who can see no joys but what are past, and fill people's heads with the unsatisfying nature of Earthly comforts', but if he did, he didn't—on this occasion—say so.[1] Nor, I think would a reading of, say, *Sonnet to the Strawberry,* or *Twilight,* justify doing so. Even Williams's *Sonnet to Hope*, though its speaker's breast 'asks not for happiness, but longs for rest', does believe in the hope that Smith's speaker has resigned, and does envisage the return of pleasure, fancy and friendship.

This is the most twilit of all Wordsworth's twilight sonnets, the first of his four so-called 'Evening Sonnets' at Cambridge:

When slow from pensive twilight's latest gleams

---

1   *Letters of Charles Lamb*, ed. Edwin W. Marrs (Cornell, 1975) 1: 144.

'O'er the dark mountain top descends the ray' [1]
That stains with crimson tinge the water grey
And still, I listen while the dells and streams
And vanish'd woods a lulling murmur make;
As vesper first begins to twinkle bright
And on the dark hillside the cottage light,
With long reflexion streams across the lake.—
The lonely grey-duck, darkling on his way,
Quaakes clamorous—deep the measur'd strokes rebound
Of unseen oar parting with hollow sound,
While the slow curfew shuts the eye of day—
Sooth'd by the stilly scene, with many a sigh
Heav's the full heart—nor knows for whom, or why—

We may be in the province of Gray, and Bowles and Williams, and prospectively Hardy, rather than anything we would very confidently call 'Wordsworth', but in this sonnet, unlike Smith's there is a sense of things sought, and things received; an interaction and a kind of blessing, and even, in that remarkable coinage 'quaakes' (which is not a misprint and presumably requires to be said with a kind of extended quaver on the 'a' in quacks!) good humour. The observer is construing, intuiting, and quietly delighting in the exploration of a scene and a mood which (the language shows) is known to be shared with other poetical observers. A decade later, the great miscellaneous sonnets of 1802 will grow from this stock—the observer watching and listening, co-creating with the scene some psychological insight, reaching towards something grander than one expects to find in sonnet form. The final line imports a surprising shift, an interpretive crux, and to my mind sounds remarkably Tennysonian, anticipatory of 'Tears, idle Tears' (itself inspired by *Tintern Abbey*), in which those tears, from some unknown depth, 'rise in the heart / And gather to the eyes', which poem is perhaps the Victorian apotheosis of the line of sensibility.

I have already quoted Williams's *Sonnet to Hope* and Wordsworth's 'Calm is all nature' and I apologise for recycling them at this point:

---

1   Modified from line 3 of Williams's 'To Twilight', quoted above, page 43.

O, ever skilled to wear the form we love!
To bid the shapes of fear and grief depart;
Come gentle Hope! With one gay smile remove
The lasting sadness of an aching heart.
Thy voice, benign Enchantress! let me hear;
Say that for me some pleasures yet shall bloom,—
That Fancy's radiance, Friendship's precious tear,
Shall soften, or shall chase, misfortune's gloom.
But come not glowing in the dazzling ray,
Which once with dear illusions charm'd my eye,—
O! strew no more, sweet flatterer! On my way
The flowers I fondly thought too bright to die;
Visions less fair will soothe my pensive breast,
That asks not happiness, but longs for rest!

Calm is all nature as a resting wheel.
The kine are couched upon the dewy grass;
The horse alone, seen dimly as I pass,
Is cropping audibly his later meal:
Dark is the ground; a slumber seems to steal
O'er vale, and mountain, and the starless sky.
Now, in this blank of things, a harmony,
Home-felt, and home-created, comes to heal
That grief for which the senses still supply
Fresh food; *for only then, when memory*
Is hushed, am I at rest. My Friends! restrain
Those busy cares that would allay my pain;
Oh! leave me to myself, nor let me feel
The officious touch that makes me droop again.

This poem, though its drafts long precede the supposed discovery of
Milton in 1802 (a version of it was published in the *Morning Post*
three months before that supposed discovery) illustrates particularly
well Wordsworth's belief that the sonnet needs the unity of 'an orbicular body' 'a dew-drop' or perhaps (for that matter) a passionate tear.
There is neither an octave nor a quatrain in the composition, though
one could call the first six lines an irregular sestet. The sentence
occupying most of the last four lines (can one call *ccac* a quatrain?)

must, one feels, somewhere have a model in Williams. It is clearly composed out of a sibling sensibility to that of her *Sonnet to Hope*. So close, indeed, is the tone and the sensibility of this Cambridge sonnet to the Williams one he recited from memory in 1820, that—it seems to me—just as one can splice the balladic lyricism of *Eltruda* and *Lucy*, or the tetrameters of *An Evening Walk* and *Peru*, one might be unsurprised to encounter a poem such as this:

> But come not glowing in the dazzling ray,
> Which once with dear illusions charm'd my eye,—
> O! strew no more, sweet flatterer! On my way
> The flowers I fondly thought too bright to die;
> ...   for only then, when memory
> Is hushed, am I at rest. My Friends! restrain
> Those busy cares that would allay my pain;
> Oh! leave me to myself, nor let me feel
> The officious touch that makes me droop again.

This poem has no existence outside the present book, yet it makes perfectly acceptable sense. It also has a surprising unity of tone and timbre, considering that four lines are from Williams's *Sonnet to Hope* (published in 1790 and recited by Wordsworth to its author thirty years later), and the rest from her admirer's *Written in Very Early Youth*, written at Cambridge and published in 1802.

3. Wordsworth (Fox) and Jeffrey: 'Namby-Pamby', or the Shock of the New?

> Mr Scott ... has chosen to copy the language of barbarous ages; it was reserved for Mr Wordsworth to imitate the lisp of children
> —*Le Beau Monde*

> What will any reader or auditor out of the nursery say to such namby-pamby as 'Lines written at the foot of Brother's Bridge'?
> —Lord Byron

Not even Keats was treated as badly by the reviewers, or in such gendered terms, as Wordsworth in 1807. Why, one has to wonder, did Wordsworth not see that devoting the larger part of his *Poems, in Two Volumes* to even more daringly humble topics than appeared in *Lyrical Ballads*, while indulging in a yet more unbuttoned display of 'getting in touch with his feminine side', was a bad move? That his reputation would not recover until he expiated all this plain language and naked sensibility in the ultra-stoicism of *The Excursion*? And why, in any case, were namby-pambiness, affectation, and childishness, perceived as the dominant traits of a publication that included the *Ode, Resolution and Independence*, and some magnificent elegies and those 'manly' (Lucy Aikin's epithet) political sonnets?

Poems, in Two Volumes and Charles James Fox

In attempting an answer—it will be a very roundabout answer—I want to begin with a not-too-challenging piece of historicism. *Poems in Two Volumes* is—quite egregiously—a war-time product. By 1807 England had been at war with France for thirteen years, with a brief intermission in 1802, the Peace of Amiens, during which Wordsworth reached his own treaty with Annette Vallon, and saw his daughter for the first time. It would remain at war (given the failure of Fox's attempts to secure an honourable peace in 1806) until Waterloo. Some of the most moving 'scenes' or moments in volume one are associated with the English Channel, and gazing across from one coast to the other, confounding patriotic with familial feelings.

The same confusion is addressed in the strangest of the so-called Lucy poems, 'I travelled among unknown men', in which one cannot be entirely sure whether the person addressed is a daughter, a sister, a lover, a wife, or England: 'Nor England, did I know till then, / What love I bore to thee'. Lucy is, in this poem, as Geoffrey Hartman pointed out, the genius loci, or the spirit of England, a spirit profoundly threatened and deeply loved. The reasons for such 'strong confusion'—Wordsworth's own term—between the personal and the historical is addressed in one of the 1807 volume's least read sonnets, which read in this context may strike one as pivotal to the entire project:

> When I have borne in memory what has tamed
> Great Nations, how ennobling thoughts depart
> When Men change Swords for Ledgers, and desert
> The Student's bower for gold, some fears unnamed
> I had, my Country! am I to be blamed?
> But, when I think of Thee, and what Thou art,
> Verily, in the bottom of my heart,
> Of those unfilial fears I am ashamed.
> But dearly must we prize thee; we who find
> In thee a bulwark of the cause of men;
> And I by my affection was beguiled.
> What wonder, if a Poet, now and then,
> Among the many movements of his mind,
> Felt for thee as a Lover or a Child.

'Beguiled' by 'affection', the poet falls into two fond and foolish thoughts, a momentary attribution to his country of the materialism of some of her inhabitants, and fear for her survival, as he would fear for a lover or a child. This is an 'If Lucy should be dead!' moment, raised to the national level and transferred to the public domain. It is rarely quoted, but in context one sees its role *as one of many poems* through which the personal and historical are constantly changing places.

Perhaps this poem, along with what I have to say in this chapter, will have some bearing on how we perceive the collection as a whole—help us to see this marriage of antipodes (the personal and the historical, the butterfly and the frozen seas; the child and England; the disconcerting—very disconcerting to early critics— juxtaposition of the 'namby-pamby' and the 'manly') as the meaning of *Poems, in Two Volumes*—both its architectural principle and its theme. *Poems, in Two Volumes*, as published, begins with one of numerous celebrations of the daisy (followed by several of the lesser celandine) and ends with the mysterious protestation (in context, this mysterious utterance is a reference back to daisies and celandines) that 'thanks to the human heart by which we live ... to me the meanest flower that blows can bring / Thoughts that do often lie too deep for tears'. If we overlook such architecture it is our oversight, not his. These lyric effusions, exploring what the daisy calls 'the homely sympathy that heeds / The common life', *enact*, it seems to me, something of what the political sonnets define as 'homely beauty', in 'the curious phrase 'the homely beauty of the good old cause', and remind one that Milton himself (who could write *Allegro* as well as *Penseroso*) asked for poetry to be not always organ-toned but also 'simple sensuous and passionate'.

The first overtly 'serious' piece in the book is a deeply thoughtful poem called *Character of the Happy Warrior*, a piece obscured by sometimes elliptical thought processes (that might have been more easily accomplished in blank verse) and by characteristically compressed syntax. A misleading endnote, published only in 1807, implies that this poem celebrates the garlanded Lord Nelson; it would be truer to say that Nelson's death led Wordsworth to ponder true greatness. Swayed from the right path by the pressures of rank and circumstance, and possibly mental alienation brought about by marital guilt, he sided with repression and hanged Admiral Caracciolo and other patriots of Naples in 1799 (as Mary Moorman put it, using some poetical licence, 'from the yard-arm of the Minerva').[1] It has been suggested by John Williams that Wordsworth may have shown his doubts about Nelson by associating him with a brutal braggart, the wife-abusing showman in *Benjamin the Waggoner* who travels about with a model of *The Victory*.[2] The likelier model of a 'Happy Warrior' is the silent poet, John Wordsworth—the indirect subject of the *Piel Castle* stanzas—who perished beneath 'the trampling wave' leaving only a 'dead unprofitable name'. Those elegiac stanzas, of course, introduce and partly explicate the *Intimations* Ode, at the end of Volume 2. This earlier poem, the *Happy Warrior*, functions as an exposition, I suggest, of the central thesis of *Poems, in Two Volumes*.

Who is the happy warrior? The answer takes five rather headlong pages. He is 'the generous spirit' loyal to 'the plan that pleased his *childish thought*', '*placable*', able to endure but, for that reason, 'alive to *tenderness*'; who can 'in himself possess his own desire'; whose 'master–bias leans / To *home felt pleasures and to gentle scenes*; / *Sweet images!*' who plays amid the games of life 'that one / Where what he most doth value must be won'. John, certainly, is one model. There may, also, be another model in this volume of a generous spirit, engaged in high endeavours, not caring too much when denied 'worldly state', and true in his way to 'his boyish plan' cleaves to one purpose and 'at the close 'sees what he foresaw'. At the close

---

1   The 1807 endnote was cancelled in all later collections and might not be known today if modern editors had not resurrected it. As Wordsworth wrote in *The Fenwick Notes*: 'Lord Nelson carried most of the virtues that the trials he was exposed to in his department of the service necessarily call forth & sustain if they do not produce the contrary vices. But his public life was stained with one great crime, so that though many passages of these lines were suggested by what was generally known as excellent in his conduct, I have not been able to connect his name with the poem as I could wish, or even to think of him with satisfaction in reference to the idea of what a warrior ought to be. For the sake of such of my friends as may happen to read this note, I will add that many elements of the character here pourtrayed were found in my brother John who perished by shipwreck as mentioned elsewhere. His messmates used to call him the Philosopher, from which it must be inferred that the qualities & dispositions I allude to had not escaped their notice, He often expressed his regret, after the war had continued some time, that he had not chosen the Naval instead of the East-India Company's Service to which his family connexion had led him.' *The Fenwick Notes*, ed Jared Curtis (Humanities-Ebooks 2007), 117.

2   John Williams, *William Wordsworth*. Critical Issues (Palgrave 2002), 117–8.

of his life in 1806, as also in 1802, Charles James Fox saw precisely what he had foreseen in 1794. At the time of the Peace of Amiens—which, if it produced nothing else did produce a beautiful sonnet to Caroline and cleared the way for Wordsworth's wedding—Charles James Fox, who had been a consistent advocate of peace, scorned the treaty and deplored its terms. Why? Because in his view, precisely the terms negotiated in 1802 could have been had in 1794 without spending the intervening years in the company of what *Character of the Happy Warrior* calls 'Pain, and Fear, and Bloodshed, miserable train'. Identifying Fox as the happy warrior may be far-fetched. But a seeming digression may explain something about these two volumes, and shed light on the anticipatory elegy for Fox, the *Lines Composed in Grasmere, during a Walk one evening after a Stormy Day, the Author having just read in a Newspaper that the Dissolution of Mr Fox was hourly expected.*

> Loud is the Vale! the Voice is up
> With which she speaks when storms are gone,
> A mighty Unison of streams!
> Of all her Voices, One!
>
> Loud is the Vale;—this inland Depth
> In peace is roaring like the Sea;
> Yon Star upon the mountain-top
> Is listening quietly.
>
> Sad was I, ev'n to pain depress'd,
> Importunate and heavy load!
> The Comforter hath found me here.
> Upon this lonely road;
>
> And many thousands now are sad,
> Wait the fulfilment of their fear:
> For He must die who is their Stay,
> Their Glory disappear.
>
> A Power is passing from the earth
> To breathless Nature's dark abyss;
> But when the Mighty pass away

What is it more than this,

That Man, who is from God sent forth,
Doth yet again to God return?—
Such ebb and flow must ever be,
Then wherefore should we mourn?

The 'Comforter' is a new and surprising note in Wordsworth's poetry, which has been profoundly changed by the death of John Wordsworth. But the glowing tribute to Fox as the people's 'Stay', 'their Glory' and 'A Power' (a portion of divine power at that) is entirely clear, and surprisingly undimmed from sentiments he might have expressed in the early 90s. Why should Fox still compel such emotively charged terms from Wordsworth in 1806?

In December 1792, William Wordsworth returned from France with the honourable intention of raising money and returning in time for the birth of his daughter. Instead he found himself, like other young men robbed, in 'one decisive rent', as he put in *The Prelude*, 'of all their pride, their joy, in England' by his country's shameful part in an anti-Gallican confederacy. It was a disaffection that lasted until, at least his second exile in Germany, in 1798/99 and, if we judge from the rhetoric of *The Prelude*, well into 1805/06 when Wordsworth was labouring to complete the full length poem and forcing himself to relive and re-assess, moment by moment, but for months on end, the meaning of the terror and of the war. On 26 January 1793 he and these idealistic youths found they were not alone. On that day, Charles James Fox, published a remarkable pamphlet: *A Letter from the Right honourable Charles James Fox to the Worthy and independent Electors of the City and Liberty of Westminster* (London 1793).

Fox's immediate subject was what might now be termed Homeland Security, questioning what on earth ministers were up to, in taking security measures 'which the law authorises only in case of insurrection within this realm' (4), namely, the sudden embodying of the militia and drawing of regular troops to the capital, and attempts to manipulate the House of Commons into endorsing such actions without proper intelligence: 'I thought it highly important, both in a constitutional and a prudential view, that the House should be thoroughly informed of the ground of calling out the militia' and argued that 'in a prudential view, surely information ought to precede judgement; and we were bound to know what really was the state of the country, before we delivered our opinion of it' (4, 7). Surely, Fox went on, 'If they saw reason to fear impending tumults and insurrections, of which the danger was imminent and pressing, ... surely the evidence of such a danger was capable of being submitted either to the House or to a secret Committee? (8) Or was it that the executive's actions 'were directed not so much to any insurrection, either actually existing or immediately impending, as to the progress of what are called French opinions ... and to the mischiefs which might in future time arise from the spirit of disobedience and disorder which these doctrines are calculated to inspire' (9). It is a prophetic passage, pointing forward to the rounding up of men like John Thelwall and their imprisonment for 'constructive treason' or, as we call it now, 'incitement to terror', when Pitt and his cronies thirsted, Wordsworth wrote in *The Prelude* 'to make the guardian crook of law a tool of murder'.

But Fox's larger theme was one to which both Robin Cook and Gordon Brown have recently given attention,[1] that of whose right it is to declare war.

> To declare war is by the Constitution, the prerogative of the King; but to grant or with-hold the means of carrying it on is (by the same Constitution) the privilege of the people, through their Representatives; and upon the people at large, by a law paramount to all Constitutions—the law of Nature and Necessity, must fall the burdens and sufferings which are the too sure attendants on that calamity. It seems reasonable therefore that they, who are to pay, and to suffer, should be distinctly informed of the object for which war is made, and I conceived nothing would tend to this information so much as an avowed negotiation, because from the result of such a negotiation, and by no other means, could we, with any degree of certainty, learn, how far the French were willing to satisfy us on all, or any of the points, which have been publicly held forth as the grounds of complaint against them....

---

1   This lecture was originally delivered at the Wordsworth Winter School in February 2007.

If in none, he argued, war would be just; if in all, we should know that the public pretences were not the real causes of the war. And 'In the last case … I should hope that there is too much spirit in the people of Great Britain, to submit to take part in a proceeding founded on deceit' (24–25).

By 1806, when Wordsworth was writing the last of his poems for these volumes, Fox was still identified as one of the, by then diminishing, anti-war party—and it is pretty clear from some of the sonnets (some of the more warlike ones belong to 1803, and one to November 1806) that Wordsworth was not. Fox was thoroughly opposed to the resumption of war after the Peace of Amiens (during which Wordsworth wrote the Calais sonnets) and he used his brief tenure in the so-called 'Ministry of all the Talents' to pursue negotiations with Napoleon, negotiations that failed with his death. The 'dissolution' of Mr Fox, the 'dissolution' of the ministry, and the 'dissolution' of any prospect for an end to war, were more or less simultaneous.

A substratum of the *Lines written in Grasmere* has long puzzled me. In 1802 Fox was one of the most distinguished of those who visited Paris to pay court to Napoleon. And we know exactly what Wordsworth thought in November 1806 of ministers in that 'venal band / Who are to judge of danger which they fear / And honour which they do not understand'. Yet it is amply clear from this poem that the emotional bond with Fox, as champion of his own early perspective on the looming war, remained unbroken. It is partly that Fox, of all parliamentarians shared most deeply Wordsworth's view of Britain's first war against liberty—the war of 1776—in which Fox, alongside Burke in those days, was Parliament's most determined advocate of the Americans: 'Liberty', I would suggest, but liberty in all its dimensions, is a consistent theme of *Poems in Two Volumes*. And it is partly that Fox, who campaigned very much on a Commonwealthman domestic agenda in the 1790s, seemed most likely to use power to a good purpose—to repay society's debt to the people whose labour was fleeced to pay for the war effort:[1] 'You', he had written to Fox in 1800, 'have felt that the most sacred property

---

1   'Sconced' was William Frend's word for it; 'sconced' a quarter of their day's pay to pay for Pitt's dubious war on liberty. *Peace and Union* (1793), 65.

is that of the poor'.

But we also know just how strained, how conflicted, and how complex were his emotions at that time. *Poems in Two Volumes* is a key moment in Wordsworth's political history. Much of his political development in the next twenty years would be driven by two related facts. In 1806 the Whigs lost by far their wisest head, and Wordsworth his last emotional tie to the Whig interest. And another of Fox's admirers, Francis Jeffrey, a man who (as I shall try to show) had every qualification to appreciate both the sanity and the bravery of *Poems in Two Volumes*, found it more amusing to make a game of holding Wordsworth up to mockery.

Francis Jeffrey on Wordsworth

As Jonathan Wordsworth says of the lyric 'The Sun has long been set', it is a poem whose 'tenderness, beauty, exuberance, have to the modern reader the unguarded charm of a Blakean song of innocence'. It does of course express the joy of William and Dorothy's homecoming, in Grasmere in 1802, and the onset of that style of life that Scott, then, and Thoreau, later, so much admired—the almost legendary retreat into a life of Homeric simplicity and austerity, remote from the business of the world, or the 'getting and spending' deplored in the great 'pagan' sonnet which (alongside the wanderer's discourse on paganism in *The Excursion*) helped to inspire the neo-classicism of Keats and Shelley.

The primary theme of Jonathan Wordsworth's introduction to his facsimile of *Poems, in Two Volumes* is 'reception study'. He dwells very appropriately on the struggles of Montgomery, a professed admirer of *Lyrical Ballads*, to come to terms with what he sees as the less focused, less serious quality of many poems in the new volumes—their lack of an evident moral purpose. Of *Lyrical Ballads* he had concluded, 'Mr Wordsworth is a living example of the power which genius possesses, of awakening unknown and ineffable sensations in the hearts of his fellow creatures'. He has 'taught us new sympathies, the existence of which in our nature had scarcely been intimated to us by any preceding poet' (Woof 208). But he was very reluctant to review *Poems in Two Volumes*, and wrote privately to the Editor of the *Eclectic* that 'The cry is up, and it is the fashion to yelp him down'. Yet 'I feel the pulse of poetry beating through every vein of thought in all compositions, even in his most pitiful, puerile and effected pieces'.[1]

It may well be true that they do not conspicuously have, as those of *Lyrical Ballads* do, 'a worthy purpose'. If so, that may be because Wordsworth in 1802 and 1806, though still troubled by 'what man has made of man', was much less angry with them. Apart from anything else, he had learned, as one of the most self-implicating of the sonnets says, to retrace 'the steps that *I* have trod' and become aware that nobody is immune to frailties. The point, of personal change for the better, is made on the very first page of Volume 1, and again in other lyrics.

The difference comes out strongly in his famous letter to Lady Beaumont. Whereas in the *Lyrical Ballads* 'Advertisement' he saw himself at war with social tendency, and certainly with the reading public, he now expresses a milder confidence that

> my writings (among them these little Poems) will co-operate with *the benign tendencies in human nature and society, wherever found*; and that they will, in their degree, be efficacious is making men wiser, better and happier.[2]

Always these triads. Wisdom, virtue and happiness; these three – and the greatest of these is *happiness*. They express an almost uniquely sunny phase in Wordsworth's life. For the next twenty years, following the chorus of execration he was about to experience, he would be bitter, defensive, jealous of praise for almost anyone else's work, and parsimonious with praise for others. But for the moment he is all geniality. Like Blake's memorable proverb, these poems 'damn braces; bless relaxes'.

James Montgomery, Jonathan Wordsworth points out, was troubled that the poet who wrote the grand lines on *The Wye* could also 'romp at random' and 'sport at large in the field of fancy'. But *The Wye* itself did little more than to spell out the faith expressed more playfully in

---

1   Robert Woof, *Wordsworth: The Critical Heritage* (Routledge, 2001), 205.
2   *Letters, MY* 1: 150, 21 May 1807.

such poems as 'It is the first mild day of Spring'. That wild, unruly and often heretical ode, however grandly marbled its blank verse, proclaims, after all, that moral life is anchored in the simplest 'language of the sense', and that even 'unremembered *pleasures* ... have no trivial influence ... on acts of kindness and of love'. That same poet has, in writing *The Prelude* (which he read aloud to Coleridge in the year he published *Poems in Two Volumes*) come to feel that even 'quaint associations' in early youth can 'impress objects' that will later 'impregnate and elevate the mind' (quaint 'associations' are the issue between him and Jeffrey, to which I will return). He has come to feel that a wiser spirit, even a benign tendency, is at work for us; and that however strange it may seem, terrors and lassitudes alike, and '*all* / The thoughts and feelings which have been infused / Into my mind' make up 'The calm existence that is mine when I am worthy of myself'. Moreover, the expressive lyrics of the two volumes function collectively (they are offered as moods, rather than poems, as if a mood were a genre) as a demonstration of *aspects* of wholeness, notes (to change the metaphor) that together compose a harmony.

One value of one value of the Woodstock edition of *Poems, in Two Volumes*, and now of Volume 1 of Jared Curtis's collection of reading texts from the Cornell volumes, is that it helps to recover Wordsworth from the obscuring effect of collected works arranged by date of composition only. *Lyrical Ballads* is more widely available in various editions which enable one to grasp the collection as it stood in 1798, or 1802 or 1805, and although the matter is little discussed, one of the most interesting features of *Lyrical Ballads* is its *architecture*. The poems in 1798 very clearly read each other, and they build in 1798 via contrasted social narratives and nature lyrics to a philosophical statement about the still sad music of humanity, and in 1800 about that one great society on earth, 'the living and the dead'. As a book, *Lyrical Ballads* is a study of human psychology—it is about how we perceive, how we make sense of our experience of nature and of others, and how personality survives, or does not survive, the stresses flesh is heir to. In 1800 the nature of the 1798 argument is enriched by the inclusion of three new genres—the Lucy elegies (about mortality), the poems on the naming of places (about what might be called personal geography), and the two great pastoral poems which focus on the imagination and sensitivity to be found in men like shepherds and sailors, in *The Brothers* and *Michael* (the two poems which Wordsworth commended especially to Fox, the people's 'Glory' and 'Stay').

It was this aspect of *Lyrical Ballads*, of course, that *permanently* prejudiced a certain witty worldling, the common sense philosopher and Scotch advocate Francis Jeffrey, against Wordsworth. At least in public. One can see Jeffrey's reading of *Lyrical Ballads* as a fatal encounter between a nominally radical Whig and a practising Democrat. Jeffrey felt personally insulted at the very notion that the feelings of a serving wench could be compared to those of a gentleman, could be in any sense *the same feelings*: the manifesto enshrined in the *Old Cumberland Beggar*, that 'we have all of us one human heart' he took as a personal insult. Since the *Edinburgh Review* was not in existence when *Lyrical Ballads* was published Jeffrey took his first bite of them while ostensibly reviewing Southey's *Thalaba* in 1802. From that point on, as he boasted, he lost no opportunity to return to the attack. He treated *Poems in Two Volumes*, *The Excursion*, *The White Doe*, and the late tours alike to sustained derision—even performing some service to Wordsworth's reputation by quoting some self-evidently sublime passages about the Pedlar's early life as if they were self-evidently absurd. But that is far from all. He found time to savage Wordsworth when Reviewing *Madoc* (1805), Crabbe's *Poems* (1808), a posthumous edition of *The Reliques of Robert Burns* (1809), *The Borough* (1810), *Kehama* (1811), and John Wilson's *Isle of Palms* (1812). You cannot say he shirked his duty. He took it very seriously indeed.

Wordsworth and Jeffrey were, one tends to suppose, poles apart in sensibility, and born to enmity. It ought to shed light on what animated the critical onslaught simply to enumerate some of their incompatibilities.[1] But Russell Noyes (sixty years ago) and Philip Flynn (in 1978) collated ample evidence that this is not really so, and

---

1   In what follows I am much indebted, apart from the primary sources, to Russell Noyes, *Wordsworth and Jeffrey in Controversy*, Humanities Series No 5 (Bloomington: Indiana University, 1941) and to Philip Flynn, *Francis Jeffrey* (Newark: University of Delaware Press; Associated University Presses, 1978).

that impression is enhanced by recent work on Jeffrey's travel dia-
ries. Like Wordsworth, Jeffrey delighted in nature, and the more so,
the more natural it was. He is a little more self-consciously painterly
perhaps, as on this walk, in 1800, from Luss to the ferry:

> It is little more than three miles from Luss to the ferry — but they
> are worth all the other miles we have come — [...] the heavy
> clouds overhung the lake and rested on the mountain tops with
> a sober sublimity that was quite in unison with the character of
> the landscape itself — [...] we had a terrific view of the moun-
> tains we were leaving — the sky was so heavy and dark over
> head that the rugged summits assumed a deep black hue and the
> clouds rolled along them like enflamed smoke on a mountain of
> wet charcoal — it really looked most horribly sublime.[1]

When he pens this lovely note about revisiting Loch Lomond, on the
same tour, he seems to have been reading *The Poem upon the Wye* (as
my italics are intended to suggest):

> two or three solitary farm houses stuck on the roots of the dreary
> mountains to our right attracted me in an unaccountable manner
> — they were little cottages *green to the very door* — no road nor
> cart nor plough nor any sign of laborious or social cultivation
> was to be seen around them — but open meadows sloped down
> in the front and smooth hills towered up to the clouds behind —
> *calm smoke went up from the green thatch* — cattle were brows-
> ing before the door and sheep *hanging* on the steep above —
> there was a dead silence — and the sun beams slept as sweetly as
> ever the moon did in the calm and desolate breast of an autumnal
> lake in a region destitute of inhabitants. (Perkins, 68)

On tour Jeffrey was inclined to throw himself on the ground, like
Tennyson later, to examine the minuter properties of flowers and he
took delight, as Wordsworth did, in what others might find uncom-
fortable weather. This is from a letter of 1822:

> It rained almost every day while we were in the highlands, and
> most commonly all day; but the weather never confined [us] for

---

1   Pamela Perkins, ed., *Francis Jeffrey's Highland and Continental Tours*,
   Humanities-Ebooks, 2009, 52.

an hour, and I do not think at all interfered with our enjoyment. It was soft, and calm, and balmy, and we walked and rowed and climbed and scrambled without minding the rain any more than the ravens.... We were out eight or nine hours every day, thoroughly wet most of the time, and never experienced the least inconvenience or discomfort, but came home more plump and rosy than we had been since last year. *The roaring of the mountain torrents in a calm morning after a raining night* has something quite delicious to my ears.[1]

Notice here (again in my italics) how Jeffrey uses the Wordsworthian image that unites *Lines written in Grasmere* (a poem he is especially likely to have appreciated because of its tribute to Fox) and *Resolution and Independence*.

Politically, Jeffrey thought Britain and France equally guilty in the nineties, and equally at fault before the Peace of Amiens and he was troubled by the resumption of hostilities—the Consulate was outrageous and provoking but he did not think Britain had the power to humble him (Wordsworth's sonnets are not especially sure of that, either). Nevertheless, like his friend Sir Walter Scott, and Wordsworth, he enlisted in the local militia and prepared to slay as many Frenchmen as he could. Seeing France's martial ardour as very much the product of English and Prussian hostility, he feared for the result of any conflict between the French—'all bone and muscle'— and the 'corpulent indolence' of England and her allies.[2] Despite such combative imagery he prized the homelier virtues. One of the things he admired about Fox was his amiable sensibility to all the kind and domestic affections, and a sort of soft-heartedness towards the sufferings of individuals'. Fox's character, he thought, like the *Happy Warrior* (which he doesn't mention) surprises us with 'traits of almost feminine tenderness'.[3]

The conflict of emotions expressed by Wordsworth in the political sonnets and in some degree shared by both men, was briefly relieved

---

1   Henry Lord Cockburn, *Life of Lord Jeffrey with a selection from his Correspondence*, 2 vols, Edinburgh 1842, 1: 212.

2   Cited from Philip Flynn, *Francis Jeffrey* (Newark: University of Delaware Press; Associated University Presses, 1978), 105

3   Francis Jeffrey, *Contributions to the Edinburgh Review* 4 vols, 1844, 2: 5.

by the rising of the Spanish against occupation and some of Jeffrey's most eloquent prose, like Wordsworth's, was devoted to the peninsula wars. For anyone unfamiliar with Wordsworth's eloquence in the *Convention of Cintra*—and its surprisingly democratic sentiments— this passage from Jeffrey gives a flavour of it:

> The people, then, and, of the people, the middle, and, above all, the lower orders, have alone the merit of raising this glorious opposition to the common enemy of national independence. Those who has so little of what is commonly termed *interest* in the country,—those who had *no stake* in the community…– the persons of no consideration in the state—they who could not pledge their fortunes, having only lives and liberty to lose,— the bulk,—the mass of the people—alone, uncalled, unaided by the higher classes … raised up the standard of insurrection … a cheering example to every people.[1]

It is Jeffrey, but it might well be Wordsworth. Sympathy for Spain helped to resolve the quandary of a man who was by no means comfortable supporting a Tory administration's policy towards France, yet who felt the call of patriotism. By 1814, like some of Wordsworth's Waterloo odes and the political sonnets, Jeffrey's prose had become almost triumphalist:

> It is a proud and honourable distinction to be able to say that, in the end of such a contest, that we belong to the only nation that has never been conquered; — to the nation that set the first example of successful resistance to the power that was desolating the world,—and who always stood erect, though she sometimes stood alone, before it. … She has set a magnificent example of unconquerable fortitude and unalterable constancy.[2]

Jeffrey's new patriotism went hand in hand, however, with a deep sympathy, parallel to that expressed in *The Excursion*, for the fate of those caught up in factory life. He was convinced that thanks to free market conditions and the accumulation of capital there was developing 'a fixed and degraded *caste* [of operatives] out of which no

---

1   *Edinburgh Review* 13, Oct 1808.
2   *Contributions*, 4: 47.

person can hope to escape who once been enrolled among its members'. While no Marxist, he perceived that middle class prosperity and education were enjoyed at the expense of the labouring poor. But there was a disabling reservation. Like Wordsworth, Jeffrey could not conceive of any 'humane remedy that would not endanger the security of private property'.[1]

Both, then, spent their middle years in a hopeless state of ambivalence about aristocracy. On the one hand, the antiquity and stability of government had many advantages. On the other, 'there is an oligarchy of great families—borough-mongers and intriguing adventurers—that monopolizes all public activity, and excludes the mass of ordinary men... How can you hope to bring the virtues of the people to bear on the vices of the government when the only way in which a patriot can approach to the scene of action is by purchasing a seat in Parliament?' (Coburn, 110). Yet by 1810, rather earlier than Wordsworth, Jeffrey starts talking about the English constitution as 'that magnificent fabric' and claiming that 'the rights and liberties of the people are best maintained by a regulated hereditary monarchy, and a large, open, aristocracy'[2] Later, Jeffrey's latent republicanism or Commonwealthman principles made him look more and more to America as the power most likely to resolve the developing crisis between liberty and order. Wordsworth was a little less optimistic, despite his American connections, about interventions from that mercantile quarter.

As for literature, Jeffrey's instincts could be radical, even levelling: it is the business of poetry, he thought, to force us 'to attend to objects that are usually neglected, and to enter into feelings from which we are in general but too eager to escape'. That could come verbatim from Wordsworth's letter to John Wilson. Most of us are capable of some sympathy with the poor, Jeffrey argued, but such impulses are unfortunately passing. What the poet can and should do is use his art to revive in our hearts those 'abortive movements of compassion, and embryos of kindness and concern, which had once fairly begun to live and germinate'. And here the metaphors 'abortive' and

1   Flynn, 133, 92.
2   *Edinburgh Review*, 15, Jan 1810.

'embryos' do sound strikingly un-Wordsworthian even if the psy-chology is not dissimilar. Yet the profile I have so laboriously accu-mulated in the last three pages—from the soft highland rains, through the Spanish rising, to those embryos of human kindness—suggests a man born to promote the recognition of Wordsworth's genius as Ruskin did for Turner's. But the praise for the poetry of common life comes from Jeffrey's 1810 review of Crabbe's *The Borough*, a review almost designed, one feels, to turn the knife in Wordsworth's flesh.

So wherein lay the irreconcilable difference? Possibly nowhere. As Scott wrote to Anna Sewall (10 April 1806) 'I have often [wondered] that a man who loves and admires poetry so much as he does ... ful-minates against the authors whom he most approves of, and whose works actually afford him most delight. But what shall we say?' Brilliantly, Scott answers his own question: 'Many good-natured country Tories (myself for example) take great pleasure in coursing and fishing, without any impeachment to their amiabilities, and prob-ably Jeffrey feels the same instinctive passion for hunting down the bards of his day.'[1] Southey suspected likewise. We can also suspect that he feels insufficiently confident in his manliness to risk associa-tion with lisping affectedness. And in truth, Jeffrey was a barrister: he was paid to tell lies to accomplish an end, in this case sales of the *Edinburgh*; like any debater, he enjoyed getting up a case on either side of any question, and he relished his own wit. Nevertheless, one can identify some predisposing factors, of a kind to push him into an adversarial stance towards *Poems, in Two Volumes*, and each of them says something significant about the critic and the collection.

First, Francis Jeffrey shared with many metropolitan critics and with Lucy Aikin, a feeling that Wordsworth was damaging his art by living in seclusion, because poetry was necessarily social not in the sense of being concerned with human society but in the quite dif-ferent sense of being part of genteel society. Jeffrey being brought up in the Scottish Enlightenment, would have agreed in theory with David Hume and with Wordsworth that 'there is a great uniformity among the actions of all men, in all nations and ages, and that human nature remains the same in its principles and operations' (*Enquiry*

---

1   *Familiar Letters of Sir Walter Scott*, Edinburgh 1894, 2 vols, 1: 41.

Concerning Human Understanding) but, as Flynn points out, he would also have agreed with Thomas Reid that 'man … is made not for the savage and solitary state, but for living in society' (*Essays on the Active Powers*), and with Adam Ferguson that 'if the palace be unnatural, the cottage is so no less' (*Essay on the History of Civil Society*).[1] The proper state of nature, as it were, is found in the drawing rooms of Edinburgh not among the fells.

Second, he was generally a determined opponent of experiment, at least in public, as evidenced in his notorious remark in the review of Southey's *Thalaba* (the occasion for his first onslaught on *Lyrical Ballads*) that 'Poetry has this much, at least, in common with religion, that its standards were fixed long ago, by certain inspired writers whose authority it is no longer lawful to call into question' [*ER* 1, Oct 1802]. Whether he genuinely held to the fixed standards of taste that he promulgates so staunchly in his reviews is another matter, however. Writing to Ugo Foscolo, who did, it seems, believe that the principles of taste were 'precise and certain', Jeffrey commented: 'That many things are certainly bad may indeed be affirmed with tolerable safety—but for my own part I never can be quite sure that what appears to me good, may not have that effect in consequence of some whim or prejudice of my own.'[2] Lacking self-reliance, Jeffrey preferred—in Scott's metaphor—to hunt with the pack.

Third, like many others—including Coleridge—Jeffrey was unpersuaded by the notion that there was any value in the notion that the language of the middle and lower orders of society can be fitted to poetry. As Jeffrey rejoined, in his very first review of Wordsworth, 'the language of the higher and more cultivated orders may fairly be presumed to be better than that of their inferiors'. It is not impossible for a man of low birth to write, but in order to write, a man of the lower orders must prune his language of errors and improprieties, and observe all the appropriate graces of prosody, and when he has done so, 'it may not be very easy to say how we are to find him out to be *a low man.*' 'A *low* man'! In the remarkable review of Burns—remark-

---

1   I merely summarise Philip Flynn's argument here; see Flynn 71–3.
2   *The letters of Francis Jeffrey to Ugo Foscolo*, ed. J Purves (London: Oliver and Boyd, 1934), p. 28 (May 1818).

able mainly for one of his most gratuitous assaults on *Alice Fell* and other affronts to superior taste—Jeffrey is generally concerned to raise Burns and depress Wordsworth, until he stumbles across this same problem of 'lowness', which divides him from Burns, too: 'we can see no propriety in regarding the poetry of Burns chiefly as the wonderful work of a peasant, and thus admiring it much in the same way as if it had been written with his toes; yet there are peculiarities in his works which remind us of *the lowness of his origin....*'.[1] Literature, to Jeffrey, is a pursuit for gentlemen. He thus takes particular exception to Burns's 'perpetual boast of his independence, ... The sentiment itself is noble, and it is often finely expressed; —but a *gentleman* would have only expressed it when he was insulted or provoked.'

Fourth, there were, in practice, limits to Jeffrey's professed interest in the poetry of common life. A Whig, rather than a democrat, he felt he knew all he needed to know about the poor. And in relation to the poor and simple (*for* whom Jeffrey was capable of feeling, though he could not feel *with* them) it seemed obvious to Jeffrey that what we already know is all we need to know. 'We all live surrounded by the poor ... and their toils, their crimes, or their pastimes, are our hourly *spectacle*. ....everyone understands about cottages, streets, and villages; and conceives, pretty correctly, the character and condition of sailors, ploughmen and artificers'.[2] What makes Crabbe palatable, according to an earlier review of the *Poems* (1808) is first that his peasants are no better than they ought to be—they do not disconcert us with the possibility that they might be our equals—and secondly that they are depicted with 'such traits of moral sensibility, of sarcasm, and of useful reflection, as everyone must feel to be natural and own to be powerful'.

Fifth, there is a concrete technical disagreement, especially pertinent to *Poems, in Two Volumes*. The theoretical justification of Jeffrey's critique is this: if a man wants to write 'he must be cautious to employ only such objects as are the natural signs and inseparable concomitants of emotions, of which the greater part of mankind are susceptible; and his taste will then deserve to be called bad and false

---

1   *Contributions*, 2: 392.
2   *Contributions*, 3: 27, on Crabbe, *The Borough* (1810). .

if he obtrude upon the public as beautiful, objects that are not likely to be associated in common minds with any interesting impressions' [*ER* 18, May 1811]. He made the same point in almost every review of Wordsworth. He might have plagiarized the point—*in fact he probably did*—from Wordsworth himself in his 1800 Preface. 'I am conscious', writes Wordsworth, in an astute piece of self-criticism,

> that my associations must have sometimes been particular instead of general, and that, consequently, giving to things a false importance, I may sometimes have written upon unworthy subjects ... Hence I have no doubt that, in some instances, feelings, even of the ludicrous, may be given to my Readers by expressions which appeared to me tender and pathetic....

but, he goes on, he would not alter such expressions on the authority of a few individuals, for fear of losing confidence in himself, and 'To this it may be added that the critic ought never to forget that he is himself exposed to the same errors as the Poet'.

And to his very great credit—his exceedingly great credit—Wordsworth, in a letter to Southey in January 1808, fresh from reading Jeffrey's review, took up the point. Both agree on the ground of associationism. Jeffrey would grasp the view of associationist aestheticians that what we call 'beauty' is not a property of objects, but consists in the feelings which arise in association with particular objects (or images). An evening sky, for instance, may suggest the calm of age, or the blessings of maturity. Or an explicitly virtuous elderly lady, provided that we are quite sure she is one of the *deserving* poor, may associate such feelings with those of benevolence. Jeffrey's one solid point, Wordsworth says, is that 'I have connected my lofty or tender feelings with objects, such as a Sparrow's nest, a Spade, a leech-gatherer, etc., which to the generality of mankind appear, and will continue to appear, ridiculous.' Does Wordsworth object to this? Well, yes and no.

> Now Mr Jeffrey takes this for granted, which was the thing to be proved; and then proceeds to revile the poems accordingly. That, to a great many persons, many objects such as I have written upon will be either unknown, indifferent or uninteresting, or

even contemptible there can be no doubt,

This might seem to be an entire capitulation to the chorus of critics, except that Wordsworth goes on:

> but *I* suppose, generally speaking, that these people are, *so far*, [i.e. so far as they feel that way about common and simple aspects of nature and human nature] in a state of degradation, at least that it would be better for them if they were otherwise. Mr Jeffrey takes for granted the contrary. Here we are at issue. [Woof, 247-8].

Twenty-one years later he made almost the same point to Crabb Robinson, in a characteristic remark on hostile critics: 'I do not blame them—they write as they feel—and that their feelings are no better they cannot help' [27 January 1829].

The judgmental consequences of such principled differences are plain enough. *Alice Fell*, in which according to Jeffrey, the speaker is unproblematically the poet, was not surprisingly dismissed by Jeffrey as a piece of such 'trash' that it amounts to 'an insult to the public taste'. It offended by its interest in low life, by its failure to select interesting facets of such low life, by its plainness of diction, by the sheer impossibility, for a gentleman, of connecting any interesting associations with a tattered cloak, and perhaps above all, by *the absence of any useful reflection or display of moral sensibility or sarcasm*. Hardly anyone until A. C. Bradley had much to say for it, and hardly anyone before Don Bialostosky paid it the tribute of skilful and illuminating analysis.[1] And one cannot really blame them.

Poetry had not hitherto expected its readers to ask such questions as 'who is speaking?', or 'is the speaker to be trusted in his appraisal of the situation?', or 'do his remarks and conclusions reach the heart of the matter?'—let alone to question such things as the benign gentleman's tone of appropriation of the child ('My child'), or his apparent inability to grasp that the child may well be frightened and is certainly more deeply alone than he can imagine. The self-satisfactions of middle class philanthropy, already explored in *Simon Lee*,

---

1   Don Bialostosky, *Making Tales: The Poetics of Wordsworth's Narrative Experiments* (University of Chicago Press, 1984), 138–43.

were not to early nineteenth century readers self-evidently problem-
atic and it is highly unlikely that many readers would find time to
admire the child's canniness (in remaining quiet when the coach is
first stopped); or appreciate her alarm at discovery; or her dignity in
responding to his patronizing manner. It is not for a child, least of all
a poor one, to stand thus on her dignity: 'My name is Alice Fell. / I'm
fatherless and motherless. / And I to Durham sir, belong'. The notion
that the bathos of the ending—the patness of the speaker's self-con-
gratulation (based, clearly, on mere conjecture, or fantasy, since his
patronage has been exercised at arm's length)—might be intended to
provoke reflection on the efficacy of such measures does not seem to
have occurred to anyone for almost 180 years.

Lucy Aikin, interestingly, who wrote the most thoughtful of generally hostile reviews, grouped *Alice Fell*, *The Leech Gatherer*,
Beggars and *The Sailor's Mother* together as 'feeble, unimpressive
and intolerably prolix' (Woof, 220). 'Fidelity' she found cold: one
might object strongly to this faintly ludicrous poem on other grounds,
but the problem for Lucy Aikin is that it didn't express enough *compassion* for the man or his dog. Without signposts, she cannot work
out at all what the point of *Alice Fell* might be. It is a reminder, I
think, that even if Wordsworth had published *The Ruined Cottage* at
an earlier date it is not at all certain that people would have known
how to take it—Wordsworth is already relying on the objective cor-
relative, as T. S. Eliot would call it, whereby the image is expected
to give rise to the appropriate feeling in the responsive reader. In
Wordsworth's case, however, he goes well beyond the conventional
range of 'associations' which his readers had with such images. In
1798 he wrote of a woman with 'a scarlet cloak' and slowly teased
out the sheer wrongness of interpreting a scarlet cloak in too thought-
less a fashion. In the 1807 volume he asks readers to generate *in
themselves* an adequate response to a ragged one, which be it what it
may, is yet the anchor of a young girl's wintry life.

Interestingly, however, Francis Jeffrey did like the most overtly
Annette-related poem in Wordsworth's oeuvre, the fascinating *Once
in a lonely hamlet*. He refers approvingly to what he sees as 'sweet
and amiable verses on a French lady separated from her own chil-

dren' (Woof 192), presumably because it dramatizes (at least ostensibly) the feelings of a woman. The richest of all Wordsworth's expressions of empathy with motherhood, *Once in a lonely hamlet* pursues the exploration of maternal feelings begun in 1798 in *The Complaint of a Forsaken Indian Woman*, in which the speaker witnesses the departure of her child as she lies awaiting death, and continued in *Her Eyes are Wild*, in which the dependency of unstable mind upon the comfort she derives from her nursing infant is the astonishingly intimate burden, and amplified in *The Affliction of Margaret*, whose eleven heart-rending stanzas explore would it would be to spend 'seven years' with 'No tidings of an only child'.

In *Once in a lonely hamlet* the emigrant mother desires to pretend for 'one little hour' that this English child is hers. Her desire may be contrasted with the aged Matthew's courage in *The Two April Mornings* when, having learned to deal with loss, he can see a young woman who reminds him of that loss and yet 'not wish her mine'. In her whispered dialogue with a borrowed child, the mother is troubled by her own actions, and guiltily unable to find the self-command she knows she needs. She knows that her tears both burden and perplex the borrowed infant, yet she needs 'to call thee by my darling's name' so that for a while, at least 'My heart again is in its place'. The temptation becomes plainest and most acute at the close:

> —I cannot help it—ill intent
> I've none, my pretty Innocent!
> I weep—I know they do thee wrong,
> These tears—and my poor idle tongue.
> Oh what a kiss was that! my cheek
> How cold it is! but thou art good;
> Thine eyes are on me— they would speak,
> I think, to help me if they could.
> Blessings upon that quiet face,
> My heart again is in its place!
>
> While thou art mine, my little Love,
> This cannot be a sorrowful grove;
> Contentment, hope, and Mother's glee,
> I seem to find them all in thee:

> Here's grass to play with, here are flowers;
> I'll call thee by my Darling's name;
> Thou hast, I think, a look of ours,
> Thy features seem to me the same;
> His little Sister thou shalt be;
> And, when once more my home I see,
> I'll tell him many tales of Thee.

The bare typography, of course, gives no impression at all of the varieties of intonation that the variety of passions treated in the poem require of the involved reader (at least, of a reader who grasps that Wordsworth's art is *dramatic*); each punctuation mark signals a shift of pace and pitch and tone to a reader who attends to what is happening. One could make a small anthology of Wordsworth's poems exploratory of motherhood, and all in the first person, of which this is in some ways the most personal, and yet also the most dramatized. It is impossible for the modern reader, biographies of the poet at hand, not to suppose that the poet—who, when he met her in Calais had been *severed from Caroline for all her fourteen years*—knew all about such temptations as felt by the emigrant mother. Jeffrey, however, would not have known that the poem he admired is one of a quartet of poems in which Wordsworth's own loss is not merely translated 'from the French' as it were, but transgendered, and had he guessed, heaven knows what he would have made of that.

For Wordsworth, war meant severance from his lover and their child, and a tendency to find both of them within himself; it also precipitated an awareness that is most focused in the *Happy Warrior* and the paradoxical sonnet to Napoleon, a conflict of sensations almost without a name, in which he finds it manly and honourable to stiffen the sinews and summon up the blood against Napoleon precisely because the said Napoleon was neither childlike nor womanly enough to be termed either manly or 'wise'. Not surprisingly, perhaps, one of the patterns that runs through both volumes is the value of nostalgia for childhood—what D. H. Lawrence, in *Piano*, called finding one's 'manhood cast down in a flood of remembrance'—and another—particularly I think in the opening suite of poems in Volume 2, is the subtle contrasting of male and female principles in the first six poems: in *Rob Roy's Grave* and *The Solitary Reaper*, *Stepping Westward* and *Glen-Almain*, *The Matron of Jedborough* and *The Highland Girl*, the noble dead may be male but the noble living are all female.

As I argued in *Wordsworth's Bardic Vocation*,[1] from the moment that Wordsworth decided to close *The Prelude* by using beauty to temper the sublime, he could be described as embarked on a gender-revision project. The questing hero of *The Prelude* is made imperfect in himself, that poem concludes, and requires finishing by the sororal and the fraternal—that is, the love of Dorothy and Coleridge—thus 'soften[ing] down / This oversternness'.[2] His metaphor is the 'softening down' of a rock-like nature to make space for the flora and fauna of feminine sensibility. The interrogation of manliness, and the promulgation of a view of manliness that is a sort of secular version of the Christ-like, takes place most conspicuously in *Poems in Two Volumes*, in such poems as *Once in a lonely hamlet* (March 1802); *Great men have been among us* and *I grieved for Buonaparte* (1802); *The Happy Warrior* (1805–1807); *The Matron of Jedborough*, and *Song at the Feast of Brougham Castle* (1807)—which Scott persuaded Jeffrey to like; and *The Horn of Egremont Castle*, for its emphasis upon magnanimity and its exhibition of competitiveness as the very antithesis of 'the happy warrior' (a theme Wordsworth revisited much later in the Milton-inspired *Artegal and Elidure*).

But inconspicuously it takes place also in those poems that gave most contemporary critics the most trouble: the 'infantile', 'puerile', 'namby-pamby' and 'effeminate' addresses to robins, daisies, kittens and butterflies. Among these, the opening address to a Daisy,

---

1   Chapter 9, '"The Milder Day"; or, Manliness and Minstrelsy'.
2   *Prelude 1805*, 13.211–68. In *1850* Mary takes her place alongside Dorothy and Coleridge in the project to temper a too exclusive attachment to the Miltonic sublime. W. J. B. Owen's 'The Descent from Snowdon', *TWC* 16:2 (1985) 65–74, sees Wordsworth renouncing, in the poem's final book, precisely the imaginative qualities that create the sublimities of *The Prelude*. One might argue that one revisionary aim of the *1850 Prelude* is to bring the sublime and the beautiful into optimum balance—as for instance in rephrasing the spots of time so as magnify the sense of terror. Thus in *1850* 'with trembling *oars* I turned' replaces 'trembling *hands*'; and elsewhere 'with the din *smitten*' puts a word of power in place of the very limp 'with the din, meanwhile'.

two delicious poems to the Celandine, and that on finding a glow-
worm, all in Volume 1, and the entire sequence of 'Moods of My
Own Mind' are delighted explorations of sensibility, exercises in
negative capability. The sequence is made up of thirteen poems, in
eleven different verse forms, with a musicality unrivalled in English
lyric: *To a Butterfly* (with its homage to Dorothy's sensibility), *The
Sun has long been set* (with its 'innocent blisses' and the cuckoo's
'sovereign cry'), *O Nightingale* (preferring the gentler stockdove to
the passionate nightingale), *My heart leaps up*, *The Cock is Crowing*
(to which I will return at the close), a rather famous poem now known
as *Daffodils*[1]and one to a circle of Snowdrops, *The small Celandine*
(muffled up from harm / In close self-shelter), *Gypsies* (somewhat
discordantly disapproving of idleness), *To a Cuckoo* (in this case a
world-transfiguring, fairyland cuckoo), *To a Butterfly* (with its breath-
takingly metaphysical simile 'not frozen seas more motionless') and
the gently wondering address to 'Hesperus' that closes the sequence.

These pansies, one might call them, because they all deepen
unexpectedly into wondering 'pensées', explore varieties of mani-
fold delight and wonder: they are little dialogues with a world that
seems bent upon our happiness, finger exercises in the kinds of claim
for sympathies between man and nature on which *The Recluse* will
depend (one almost wonders whether he was experimenting with an
imagistic version of *The Recluse*, in the hope that he could then forget
about that immense burden of 30,000 lines or more of blank verse).
In the entire sequence, only *Gypsies* strikes a false note of earnest-
ness and reproof, especially in a sequence which is generally on holiday from duty, and reading that poem in its proper context does make
one wonder whether that might—just conceivably—be its point.[2]

Such lyrics are notably in tune with the sonnet Wordsworth chose
to introduce his belated sensibility sequence, the 'Miscellaneous
Sonnets'. Compared with the grand tones that are to come, and which

---

1   'These volumes ... have excited, by turns, my tenderness and warm admira-
     tion, my contemptuous astonishment and disgust. The two latter rose to their
     utmost height when I read about his dancing daffodils', Anna Seward, Woof
     250.
2   See Heidi Thomson's pages on this poem in *Grasmere, 2009* (Humanities-
     Ebooks 2009), 126–9.

as Stuart Curran says,[1] virtually 'explode with their access to power' (as in 'and all that mighty heart is lying still', 'the sea that bares her bosom to the moon', and 'it is a beauteous evening calm and free') this particularly sonnet is curiously 'retro', looking back to the accents of the 1790s:

> How sweet it is, when mother Fancy rocks
> The wayward brain, to saunter through a wood!
> An old place, full of many a lovely brood,
> Tall trees, green arbours and ground flowers in flocks;
> And Wild rose tip-toe upon Hawthorn stocks,
> [...]
> Verily I think,
> Such place to me is sometimes like a dream
> Or map of the whole world: thoughts, link by link,
> Enter through ears and eyesight, with such gleam
> Of all things, that at last in fear I shrink,
> And leap at once from the delicious stream.

We are, as we are with 'Moods of My Own Mind', in the province of the blithe wisdom of *The Tables Turned*, Wordsworth's days being connected each to each back to the spring of 1798; but the closing lines are redolent also of the numerous provocative drafts he was composing in Alfoxden towards the unwritten, and eventually unwriteable, *Recluse*, and its 'high argument' concerning the 'excursive power / of intellect and thought', how the senses are at once 'the mind and the mind's ministers', and how 'All things shall live in us and we shall live in all things that surround us'. In a woodland trance in the *Christabel* manuscript [DC MS 15] Wordsworth then wrote of how:

> All melts away, and things that are without
> Live in our minds as in their native homes

and of sensations imaged as 'A vivid *pulse* of sentiment and thought'.[2]

---

1   Stuart Curran, *Poetic Form and British Romanticism* (Oxford University Press, 1986), 45.
2   Transcribed in James Butler & Karen Green, ed., *Lyrical Ballads and Other Poems* (Cornell, 1992), 322, 324.

Another such trance is described thus in the *Alfoxden* manuscript:

> I lived without the knowledge that I lived
> Then by those beauteous forms brought back again
> To lose myself again, as if my life
> Did ebb and flow with a strange mystery[1]

We are not as far as we might imagine, in these exploratory drafts for the philosophic poem, from our starting point in Chapter 2, the sonnet to Miss Williams. Both involve surrender, and ebb and flow:

> Life left my loaded heart, and closing eye;
> A sigh recalled the wanderer to my breast;
> Dear was the pause of life, and dear the sigh
> That called the wanderer home, and home to rest.

The sensibility inheritance was vital to the poetry and the theory of lyrical ballads; but as such transitions may show, it is not far, either, from the poetic mission of his life. And of course, for a male poet to write in such exceedingly invertebrate terms was asking for trouble. The whiff of effeminacy was strong enough to condemn even the most 'manly' content of the volumes to inattention.

Wordsworth Unmanned; or, the cost of criticism

Jonathan Wordsworth asks, very reasonably, in his introduction to *Poems, in Two Volumes,* how it could be that Jeffrey and Montgomery could not respond to the Miltonic sonnets and 'the Ode'. It was a general problem. Francis Jeffrey fails to respond at an adequate level to almost anything in these two volumes apart from *Brougham Castle*—and there he is impressed, mainly, I think, by the dramatized and ironically 'placed' voice of the traditional minstrel—where Wordsworth appears briefly in a manner approaching that of Jeffrey's lifelong friend, Sir Walter Scott, who indeed persuaded Jeffrey that this was one poem he ought to like. Why were these amazing sonnets not read; or when read, not understood? Byron, to his credit, did feel that one of them at least expressed 'sentiments, which we hope are

---

1   De Selincourt ed., *Wordsworth: Poetical Works,* 5: 341

common to every Briton in the present crisis: the force and expression is that of a genuine poet, feeling as he writes'. And for Lucy Aikin, the sonnets 'hold a severe and manly tone which cannot be in times like these too much listened to—they bear strong traces of feeling and of thought, and convince us that on worthy subjects this man can write worthily'.[1] That has the very great distinction of being the most substantial and extended remark on a sequence of poems that Wordsworth saw as, collectively, 'a poem on the subject of civil liberty and national independence, which, either for simplicity of style or grandeur of moral sentiment, is alas! likely to have few parallels in the poetry of the present day'. Many would agree with that self-assessment; they are poems which would seem to nominate themselves for any national curriculum, especially in the 19th century.

But I have written on the political sonnets in *Wordsworth's Bardic Vocation* and will not repeat myself here, except in so far as it bears on what Jeffrey chose not to say about these volumes. In my first chapter I unpacked the famous lines, 'The later Sydney [i.e. Algernon, not the sonneteer Sir Philip], Marvel, Harrington, / Young Vane and others who called Milton friend'. Did Jeffrey really fail to grasp their significance? Of course he did imply that the imitation of Milton raised Wordsworth above his usual level (though not as high as the imitated) but he offered no remark on the few sonnets he cited in reviewing *Poems, in Two Volumes* (admitting that there were numerous equally fine passages) to explain his preference. Yet in the very same year, reviewing a posthumous work by Fox, Jeffrey made some very telling remarks. There was a consensus in the 1790s, Jeffrey says, that 'the revolution of 1688, it was agreed, could not be mentioned with praise without giving some indirect encouragement to the revolution of 1789; and it was thought as well to say nothing in favour of Hamden, or Russell, or Sidney, for fear it might give spirits to Robespierre, Danton, or Marat. To this strict regimen the greater part of the nation submitted of their own accord; and it was forced upon the remainder by a pretty vigorous system of proceeding.' Fox's history is praised as likely to put an end to 'this system of timidity'.[2]

---

1   Woof, 220.
2   *Contributions to the Edinburgh Review*, 2: 12.

There is a pattern here, is there not? Crabbe is praised for writing about what most people find beneath their notice and trying to amend our feelings. Fox's feminine sensibility is found heartening. Fox's sense of history manfully puts an end to a 'system of timidity'. And Wordsworth who does all these things, which Jeffrey seriously wishes to commend? Well Wordsworth is to be hunted down.

One dimension of the significance of Wordsworth's sonnets is well expressed by Francis Jeffrey in a brilliant article of May 1820 on the continuity of republican sentiment between Washington's America and the Commonwealth tradition in England. He is reviewing a work on perceived British calumnies of America, and he attributes such calumnies to the party which supports absolute monarchy: 'That party has never forgiven the success of America's war of independence, and the spectacle of her republican prosperity 'is unspeakably mortifying to their high monarchical principles' (*Edinburgh Review*, May 1820, 400).

This sense of America as almost the last bastion of freedom and as a place of refuge and renewal is one of the most striking continuities between men like Richard Price and Joseph Priestley and Fox, Jeffrey and Wordsworth. Price's interest, of course, is in what America represents for the future of mankind, and the future of England. If the kind of union he envisaged had proved possible, 'The Liberty of America might have preserved our Liberty; and under the direction of a patriot king or wise minister, proved the means of restoring to us our almost lost constitution'. Even now, rather than an imposed subjection 'Ought we not rather to wish earnestly, that there may be at least ONE FREE COUNTRY left upon earth, to which we may fly, when venality, luxury, and vice have completed the ruin of liberty here?'[1] Wordsworth was in some respects rather cooler in his admiration for America, but he famously called Washington 'the honour of our own age ... the deliverer of the American continent'[2] and took pride in the fact that Henry Reed, his American editor was a grandson of General Joseph Reed (1741–85) Washington's friend and aide-de-camp.

---

1   Richard Price, *Observations on the Nature of Civil Liberty* (1776), 37, 40.
2   Convention of Cintra, in *The Prose Works of William Wordsworth*, ed. W. J. B. Owen and J. W. Smyser, Humanities-Ebooks, 2008, 1: 25.7

It is easy to conceive, Jeffrey argues in his review,

> that the splendid and steady success of the freest and most popu-
> lar form of government that ever was established in the world,
> must have struck the most lively alarm into the hearts of all those
> who were anxious to have it believed that the people could never
> interfere in politics but to their ruin.

But he dreads (is he giving the 'special relationship' its first authoritative utterance?) the *isolation* of America from the 'momentous con-
test impending' between the principles of Reform and Liberty and
those of 'Established Abuse'. The next fifty years will be crucial, and
the question is the Churchillian one, whether the new world will step
forth with all its power and might—(though he doesn't *quite* say that,
its 'prodigious power' is Jeffrey's term)—to help redress the balance
of the old, or whether it will 'stand aloof, a cold and disdainful spec-
tator'. It will be a tragedy if America 'should nourish such animos-
ity towards England, as to feel a repugnance to make common cause
with her, even in behalf of their common inheritance of freedom'.

The moment is at hand for the good old cause to triumph, and not
only America's *example* but her *influence* 'will be wanted in the crisis
which seems to be approaching'. It is an astonishing appeal. Jeffrey
at this point in history interprets the proper relations of England and
America in terms of a continuous political evolution which in Whig
mythology runs from the days of Henry Vane (champion of two
Commonwealths), through to the War of Independence (ignited by
Tom Paine with the ideas of Sidney and Harrington, Obadiah Hulme
and Richard Price). Although that War of Independence had failed
to lead to a third English Revolution on the same principles, its success will culminate, at some time in the nineteenth century, in the re-
assimilation by the mother country of principles exported to America
and triumphantly demonstrated there (by 'born and bred subjects of
the King of England') to be not merely operable but successful.

And where was Wordsworth by 1820? Opposing reform with all his
might and writing pamphlets justifying patronage, rotten boroughs,
and old corruption. And, for the most part, writing poetry which has
had very little to say to anyone at any time since its publication. And

why was he in that position? In part because of the reviews of *Poems, in Two Volumes*: reviews which drove him—despite his denials that he paid them any heed—into abandoning the experimental, and into a proud and jealous retreat from what Browning called 'the van'. The *Poems*—despite containing the political sonnets, *Resolution and Independence*, *The Solitary Reaper*, and *Intimations*—sold fewer than 500 copies in two years. Unable to support a family through his writing, and having no independent means, Wordsworth found himself a patron (Lord Lonsdale) from whom he accepted the distributorship of stamps, and for whom, eventually, he would write pamphlets extolling the constitution and old corruption. Burns too had accepted patronage (as a distributor of stamps, and for the infamous Pitt) and I do not recall anyone whipping him. But Wordsworth's retreat earned the disgust of Hazlitt, Shelley, Keats, further derision from Byron (a lifelong stranger to either want or responsibility) and, of course, from Jeffrey.

Wordsworth's protestations of being unmoved by criticism ('my ears are stone-dead to this idle buzz, and my flesh as insensible as iron to these petty stings', as he wrote to Lady Beaumont) are moving. They are also untrue. First he protested. Writing to Scott in January 1808 he wrote: 'In the first sentence of what he has said of my *Poems* [Jeffrey] has shewn a gross want of the common feeling of a British Gentleman. …. If Mr J continues to play tricks of this kind, let him take care to arm his breech well, for assuredly he runs desperate risque of having it soundly kicked' (*MY* 1: 192). Then he conformed. Not until his sixties does Wordsworth relax in poetry sufficiently again to compose such poems as *The Primrose of the Rock* (1831), *Love Lies Bleeding* and *A Wren's Nest* (1833), *The Red-Breast'* (1834)—the wren's nest written overtly for those 'whose minds without disdain / Can turn to little things' –and when he does so he shows that he has learned how to throw over such themes, as Jeffrey advised, 'appropriate traits … of useful reflection'. If he addresses *The Widow on Windermere Side* (1837) it is now in three sonnets of elevating discourse on honour, conscience and faith.

Critics used to speak of Wordsworth's 'great decade'; and if there was such a thing, it ended with the reception of *Poems, in*

Two Volumes. He does of course *publish* such early poems as *The Waggoner* and *Peter Bell* but the language of *The White Doe* and *The Excursion* (equally scorned by Jeffrey though now for their for their mystical ravings) is quite as elevated as he or Coleridge could wish. It is a poetic tragedy; a personal tragedy; and national one. Browning was right, with much oversimplification, and with no inkling of why Wordsworth took his 'handful of silver':

> Shakespeare was of us, Milton was for us,
>   Burns, Shelley, were with us—they watch from their graves!
> He alone breaks from the van and the freemen
>   —He alone sinks to the rear and the slaves!
>
> ...
>
> Life's night begins: let him never come back to us!
>   There would be doubt, hesitation, and pain,
> Forced praise on our part—the glimmer of twilight,
>   Never glad confident morning again

But Browning owes Wordsworth too much to maintain his anger: let him be 'pardoned in heaven', he concludes, and take his place where he belongs 'the first by the throne'.

I need not dwell on the cruelty—imperceptibly to his contemporaries but known so well to us—of the reception of volumes so deeply permeated with sorrows for the death of John Wordsworth. None could know what it cost Wordsworth, after the wreck of the Abergavenny, to write in the *Elegiac Stanzas* (Piel Castle) of the 'delusion' of 'a smiling sea', or of 'That Hulk which labours in the deadly swell', or to desire 'the unfeeling armour of old time', to brave 'The lightning, the fierce wind and [above all] 'the trampling waves'.

Such lines we all remember. But reading Wordsworth only in selections we lose sight of very different lines such as these, from the long and playfully thoughtful preamble *To the Daisy*:

> A hundred times, by rock or bower,
> Ere thus I have lain couch'd an hour,
> Have I derived from thy sweet *power*
>   Some apprehension;
> Some steady love; some brief delight;

> Some memory that had taken flight;
> Some chime of fancy wrong or right;
>> Or stray invention
>
> ...
>
> And all day long I number yet,
> All seasons through, another debt,
> Which I wherever thou art met
>> To thee am owing;
> An instinct call it, a blind sense;
> A happy, genial influence,
> Coming one knows not how nor whence,
>> Nor whither going

The rhythms are delicious; the relaxed iambics of the tetrameters, subtly differentiated with their occasional caesurae, are balanced by the slower, poised, deliberate dimeters with their feminine endings. And the diction is, as an estate agent might say, 'deceptively simple'. 'Sweet power'; 'blind sense'; 'genial influence': these paradoxes miniaturize some of the great themes of *On revisitng the Wye* and *The Prelude*. In this collection they parley with the 'magnanimous weakness', 'homely beauty' and 'inward happiness' of the sonnets.

Some lyrics in the 'Moods of my own Mind' sequence are 'barely on the threshold of a poetic event' (as someone once said of Emily Dickinson's less finished pieces) but their celebration of what *The Sun has long been set* calls 'innocent blisses' is not therefore to be scorned. They belong very clearly to the age of sensibility, but thoroughly purged of the mawkishness of Mary Robinson and Charlotte Smith. Take for instance, *Written in March, while resting on the Bridge at the Foot of Brother's Water*, a piece of apparently spontaneous joy in the relief that follows the passing of rain; nothing but rain. In its concluding line it announces in quite a different key from that of 'The Recluse' (indeed on gleeful holiday from that forlorn project), headlong, playful, rhythmic, pulsating, various, a spousal consummation of mind and world. Northrop Frye, in a pioneer essay on the poetry of sensibility, wrote of the period's indulgence in a poetry almost of free association, with rhymes begetting rhymes, in which gladness verges (as *Resolution and Independence* says it may)

upon madness: 'in the composing of poetry where rhyme is as important as reason, there is a primary stage in which words are linked by
sound rather than sense ... and in the way it operates it is very like
a dream'; such poetry, Frye concludes, is concerned 'to utter, rather
than to address' (150).[1]

That, we are endlessly told (because people read Wordsworth only
in selections, mostly rather high-minded and invariably pentameter
selections to boot), Wordsworth never does. And yet:

> The cock is crowing,
> The stream is flowing,
> The small birds twitter,
> The lake doth glitter,
> The green field sleeps in the sun;
> The oldest and youngest
> Are at work with the strongest;
> The cattle are grazing,
> Their heads never raising;
> There are forty feeding like one!
>
> Like an army defeated
> The Snow hath retreated.
> And now doth fare ill
> On the top of the bare hill;...

I pause here, momentarily, because that last line (like many in
Wordsworth) will not read itself. It makes auditory sense only if
we suppose Wordsworth to be regressing, laying aside all his polite
Cambridge education—anything that separates him from the plough-
boy with whom he shares the poem (which may be why Lord Byron
singled out this poem as 'namby-pamby'). So, reprising those last
two lines in the timbre proper to this poem, let us proceed gaily on,
slowing necessarily as the *rallentando* effect prepares for the last
line's emphatic (and biblically cadenced) declaration:

> And now doth fare ill
> *On 't top o 't bare hill;*

1   Northrop Frye, 'Towards Defining an Age of Sensibility', *ELH* 23:2 (1956) 144–
     52, 147, 150.

> The Plough-boy is whooping—anon—anon:
>> There's joy in the mountains;
>> There's life in the fountains;
>> Small clouds are sailing,
>> Blue sky prevailing;
> The rain is over and gone!

That final, unexpected, unbuttoned quotation from the joys of the Song of Solomon is almost redundant, since the mountains and fountains couplet speaks of the same erotic jouissance, as does the sleeves-rolled-up insouciance of the 'sailing ... prevailing' couplet: 'Damn braces, Bless relaxes', indeed!

Severing the Miltonic from the 'namby-pamby', I have been trying to say in this essay—and severing one part of a poet from another is what editions and anthologies invariably, unwittingly, do—hides what *Poems, in Two Volumes* was primarily about. Readers in 1807, with their highly stereotyped expectations of heavily gendered poetry, would have welcomed a stricter severance of sense from sensibility. They were bewildered by the collection's progress from addresses to the daisy to intimations of immortality, its juxtaposition of the orphan Alice Fell with the mysterious and quasi-sublime leechgatherer, its equal celebrations of Rob Roy and the Shepherd Lord on the one hand and of 'Moods of My Own Mind' on the other, and by the remarkable alternations of feeling in the Scottish poems. It is clear from the reviews collected in Robert Woof's *Critical Heritage* volume, that the overt display of sensibility in the lyrics rendered the grander poems in the collection almost invisible—a poet who 'lisps' childishly in one poem cannot expect us to bring critical intelligence to bear upon his sonnets, elegies, or odes. Yet what this sensibility-laced collection was offering, like D. H. Lawrence's kindred 'Pansies' a century later, was healing and holism, for a world at war.

Helen Maria Williams: a Select Bibliography

Peru, a poem. In six cantos, 1784*

Poems in Two Volumes, 1786*

Julia, a novel, 1790

Letters from France, 8 volumes, 1790–96

First series:

1. *Letters written in France in the Summer 1790*, 1790 (reprinted frequently 1792–96)*

2. *Letters from France, Containing Many New Anecdotes relative to The French Revolution*, 1792

3. *Letters from France...Particularly Respecting the Campaign of 1792*, Vol 3, 1793 (2nd edn 1796).

4. *Letters from France...Particularly Respecting the Campaign of 1792*, Vol 4, 1793 (2nd edn 1796).

Second Series:

5–6. *Letters Containing a Sketch of the Politics of France from the Thirty-first of May 1793, till the Twenty-eighth of July 1794 and of the Scenes which have passed in the Prisons of Paris*. 2 vols. London 1795 (Volume 1 written in Switzerland in 1794, published July 95, excerpted in the *Weekly Entertainer*, taken to Racedown by Azaziah Pinney by Jan 96, read by DW in Feb 96, a copy in Rydal Mount Library)*

7. *Letters Containing a Sketch of the Scenes which passed in various departments of France during the Tyranny of Robespierre and of the Events which took place in Paris on the 28th of July 1794*, 1795. [Also published as *Memoirs of the Reign of Robespierre*]

8. *Letters Containing a Sketch of the Politics of France from the 28th of July 1794 to the Establishment of the Constitution in 1795*, 1796.

Paul and Virginia, 1795.* A translation of Bernardin Saint Pierre's *Paul et Virginie*, with original sonnets by HMW.

Poems, moral, elegant and pathetic ... and original sonnets, 1796.* This collection merely appends the sonnets from *Paul and Virginia* to works by Pope, Jerningham, Blair (The Grave), Gray (The Elegy), and Percy.

A Tour in Switzerland, 1798*—a volume which punctures the sentimental illusion of English travellers, Coleridge and Wordsworth included, that late 18th Century Switzerland was still the home of liberty (Williams's view, summarized in her later *Sketches* was that 'a sentiment of liberty certainly existed in Switzerland, tho' the forms of its government were often in contradiction to its essence', *Sketches*, 1: 22)

Sketches of the State of Manners and Opinions in the French Republic towards the close of the Eighteenth Century, 2 vols., 1801*— which reconsidered, inter alia, the French invasion of Switzerland and Nelson's behaviour in Naples.

The political and confidential correspondence of Lewis the Sixteenth; with observations on each letter, 1803.*

Narrative of the Events Which Have Taken Place in France from the Landing of Napoleon Bonaparte on the 1st March, 1815, till the Restoration of Louis XVIII. 1815, 2nd edn John Murray 1816*

On the Late Persecution of Protestants in the South of France, 1816

Letters on the Events which have passed in France since the restoration in 1815, 1819* – Dorothy Wordsworth acquired a copy of this book through Henry Crabb Robinson.

Poems on Various Subjects, 1823

Souvenirs de le Revolution Francaise, 1827—written in English, as an antidote to Royalist histories, but only published in French.

* copies of these titles are in the Jerwood Centre

Appendix: Textual Echoes

This Appendix (my lecture handout for 'Helen Maria Williams: Wordsworth's Revolutionary Anima', Grasmere 2007), offers this simple tabulation of parallels in the writings of Wordsworth and Williams, designed to demonstrate the practicability of summarising Wordsworth's account of the French Revolution in Williams's words.

Williams is cited from: *Letters from France* (8 vols 1790-96); *Memoirs of the Reign of Robespierre* (1795) *Sketches of the State of Manners and Opinions in the French Republic towards the close of the Eighteenth Century* (2 vols, 1801); *A Narrative of the Events which have taken place in France ...* (1816)

Williams:	Wordsworth:
'I who ... have witnessed all the successive phases of its revolutions, ... its calamities, its triumphs, and its crimes!' *Narrative*, 1816, p. 1	'Long time hath Man's unhappiness and guilt / Detained us....' (*Prelude* 11: 1-2)
'I arrived at Paris ...the day before the federation [the **Fête de la Fédération**] ... how am I to paint the impetuous feelings of that ... exulting multitude ... my heart caught with enthusiasm the general sympathy ...'(*Letters* 1-3). 'it is very difficult, with common sensibility, to avoid sympathising in general happiness' (*Letters* 1.1.66)	But ''twas a time when Europe was rejoiced, / France standing on the top of golden hours, / And human nature seeming born again....it was our lot / To land at Calais on the very eve of **that great federal day**; and there we saw /.../ How bright a face is worn when joy of one/ Is joy for tens of millions'
'living in France at present, appears to me somewhat like living in **a region of romance**. ...while I contemplate these things I sometimes think that the age of chivalry, instead of being past for ever, is just returned' (*Letters* 1.2.4–5)	[Beaupuy, 9: 298-302] 'He through events / Of that great change wandered in perfect faith/ As through a Book, **an old Romance** or Tale of Fairy.' [and, of course, in 'Bliss was it that dawn'] 'The attraction of **a Country in Romance**' [10: 695]

Williams:	Wordsworth:
The fate of the rich: 'Must I be told that my mind is perverted, that I am become dead to all sensations of sympathy, because I do not weep' for the rich? 1.1.218	*Llandaff*: ... 'If you should lament the sad reverse by which the [Cardinal Bishop] has been divested of about 1,300,000 livres of annual revenue, you may find some consolation that a part of this prodigious mass of riches is gone to preserve from famine some thousands of curés who were pining in villages unobserved by courts.'
Sensibility: [HMW describes the Fr leaders as] 'men well acquainted with the human heart' and 'the most powerful passions of human nature'. [They know how to awaken] "that general sympathy which is caught from heart to heart with irresistible energy" (1.1.61-62)	['To my Sister'] 'Love, now an universal birth, / From heart to heart is stealing, / From earth to man, from man to earth,— / It is the hour of feeling.'
Sight-seeing: ...the far-famed lanterne at which, for want of a gallows, the first victims of popular fury were executed, I own that the sight of *la lanterne* chilled the blood within my veins. At that moment, for the first time, I lamented the revolution ... but alas! where do the records of history point out a evolution unstained by some actions of barbarity? (1.1.80–81)	Cf Wordsworth in Paris as a tourist: 'Where silent zephyrs sported with the dust / Of the Bastille I sate in the open sun, / And from the rubbish gathered up a stone / And pocketed the relic in the guise of an Enthusiast....[9.63 ff] , and I crossed ... The Square of the Carousel, few weeks back / Heaped up with dead and dying [10.46 ff]

Williams:	Wordsworth:
Violence: 'Shall we, because the fanatics of liberty have committed some detestable crimes, conclude that liberty is an evil, and prefer the gloomy tranquillity of despots? ...The occasional evils which have happened in the infant state of liberty, are but the effects of despotism. Men have been long treated with inhumanity, therefore they are ferocious. They have often been betrayed, therefore they are suspicious. They have once been slaves, and therefore they are tyrants'. 1.2.204	'... have you so little knowledge of the nature of man as to be ignorant, that a time of revolution is not the season of true Liberty. Alas! the obstinacy &perversion of men is such that she is too often obliged to borrow the very arms of despotism to overthrow him, and in order to reign in peace must establish herself by violence.' (*Llandaff*).
Domestic Treason: Williams gives much attention to the defection of Lafayette—who, however, rather redeems himself by standing up to Napoleon at a later point—and the treason of Dumouriez who does not]	'Conscious that an enemy lurking in our ranks is ten times more formidable than when drawn out against us, that the unblushing aristocracy of a Maury or a Cazalès is far less dangerous than *the insidious mask of patriotism assumed by a La Fayette or a Mirabeau*, we thank you for your desertion.' (*Llandaff*)
Ignorance: [The declaration of the Republic, 10 August 1792] 'has been succeeded by a conflict ... between freedom and anarchy, knowledge and ignorance, virtue and vice. ... the "Commune provisoire de Paris" [has] committed more crimes than despotism itself would have achieved in ages.' 1.3.3	Compare, perhaps, 'what the people were, through ignorance / And immaturity' [10: 182-3]

Williams:	Wordsworth:
Remorselessness [Feb 93] 'The faction of the anarchists desired that the French king should be put to death without the tedious forms of a trial. This opinion, however, was confined to the summit of the Mountain, that elevated region, where, aloof from all the ordinary feelings of our nature, no one is diverted from his purpose by the weakness of humanity, or the compunction of remorse' 1.4.1	(c.f. the plot of *The Borderers*, and characterization of Rivers/Oswald, composed shortly after reading this passage)
Regicide: 'History will indeed condemn Lewis the sixteenth. The evidence of his guilt [inviting foreign armies, organising a system of bribery and corruption] is clear...But His judges also must appear at that tribunal...'1.4.9 [calls him "the unfortunate monarch" and "the unhappy monarch" as WW does in 10.42]	'If you had attended to the history of the French revolution as minutely as its importance demands, so far from stopping to bewail his death, you would rather have regretted that the blind fondness of his people had placed a human being in that monstrous situation which rendered him unaccountable before a human tribunal. ... Any other sorrow for the death of Louis is irrational and weak. In France royalty is no more; the person of the last anointed is no more also, ...' [*Llandaff*].
Louvet's denunciation [HMW also criticizes the irresolution of the good guys. Louvet himself acknowledges the support of Roland, but blames Brissot, Guadet, Pethion and Vergniaud who 'supported us but feebly' [Louvet's *Narrative*, 24].	[Louvet's denunciation of the crimes of Robespiere as early as 29 October 1792]: 'Louvet was left alone without support / Of his irresolute friends '[10.102–3]

Williams:	Wordsworth:
War: 'Whilst the cause was just, she triumphed…but when, dazzled by the splendour of her victories…she commanded where she promised support, and enslaved where she had offered independence—she became the tyrant in her turn…' (*Letters* 1.4.79; it isn't clear to what this 'when' refers but it cannot be later than 1794).	'But *now*', become oppressors in their turn, / Frenchmen had changed a war of self-defence / For one of conquest'. *Prelude* 11: 206 [It is not possible to date this 'now' with any certainty—it is likeliest to refer to May 1794]
Snakes and pigmies: [France] 'infested as she is by traitors within , and menaced by a host of foes without, she will yet be suspicious; and of suspicion ferocity is the constant attendant.…[but] we must not complain that the genius of liberty…should crush, with unrelenting step the pigmies of aristocracy or despotism which stood in its way '1.3.239-40	'The Herculean Commonwealth had put forth her arms and throttled with an infant godhead's might / The snakes about her cradle.'
Moloch: 'Upon a tribune in the centre of the theatre, Robespierre, as president of the Convention, appeared, and … this high priest of Moloch, within view of that very spot where his daily sacrifice of human victims was offered up … invoked the parent of universal nature, talked of the charms of virtue and breathed the hope of immortality.' 2.2.90 (and *Memoirs* [1795], 213)	[Prelude 10: 468-9] 'this foul Tribe of Moloch was o'erthrown / And their chief Regent levelled with the dust'

Williams:	Wordsworth:
The decree of proscription of 29 deputies [2 June 93] 'From that fatal decree may be dated all the horrors which have cast their sanguinary cloud over the glories of the revolution' (2.1.81) [i.e. neither the Sept massacres nor the execution of Louis represent a major issue for her]	[If Wordsworth had a comparable moment it was the **England's 'open war'** against liberty, roughy August 93:] 'No shock / Given to my moral nature had I known / Down to that very moment [*i.e. neither the Sept massacres nor the death of Louis constituted a comparable 'shock'*]
Pride of place given to **Mme Roland** and her famous cry 'Liberty what crimes are committed in thy name'	'The illustrious Wife of Roland felt that agony / And gave it vent in her last words' (10: 352–3)
Virtue: 'If France, during the unrelenting tyranny of Robespierre, exhibited unexampled crimes, it was also the scene of extraordinary virtue' 2.1. 211	'[I] saw in rudest men, / Self-sacrifice the firmest; generous love, / And continence of mind, and sense of right, / Uppermost in the midst of fiercest strife. (9: 386-9) [and] human nature faithful to itself under worst trials' (10: 447–8)
The Great Terror [tales of atrocity occupy two volumes of the *Letters* and inspired Carlye and Dickens. The gist is conveyed in two simple statements] 'sometimes whole generations were swept away in at one moment' (2.1.216) and 'multitudes were summoned at once... The husband was scarcely allowed time to bid his wife a last farewell, or the mother to recommend her orphan children to the compassion of such of the prisoners as might survive the general calamity' (2.2.98–99)	'Domestic carnage now filled the whole year With feast-days; old men from the chimney nook, The maiden from the bosom of her love, The mother from the cradle of her babe, The warrior from the field—all perished, all— Friends, enemies, of all parties, ages, ranks, Head after head, and never heads enough For those that bade them fall.'
Macbeth [citation of *Macbeth*, to describe the state of Paris]: "Alas poor country ... it cannot be called our mother but our grave...where sighs and groans and shrieks that rend the air are made, not marked") 2.2.66	[WW presents himself in October 92 meditating on the Sept massacres as presaging more and worse violence] 'And in such way I wrought upon myself until I seemed to hear a voice that cried, To the whole city, 'Sleep no more'. (9: 93).

Williams:	Wordsworth:
'The past seems like one of those frightful **dreams** which presents to the disturbed spirit phantoms of undescribable horror, and "deeds without a name"; awakened from which, we hail with rapture the cheering beams of the morning…' (2.1.257)	[Cf Wordsworth's much guiltier nightmares, in which he appears to plead before unjust tribunals] 'with a voice / Labouring, a brain confounded, and a sense, / Death-like, of treacherous desertion, felt / In the last place of refuge—my own soul'. (10.370 ff)
Paris: [HMW sees **Paris** as] 'the slaughterhouse of man; there chiefly were men for the most part ignorant and unenlightened…made *arbiters* of the liberty, property, and even lives of their fellow citizens' 2.1.94	'Let me then relate that now, / In some sort seeing with my proper eyes / That Liberty, and Life, and Death, would soon / To the remotest corners of the land / Lie in the **arbitrement** of those who ruled / **The capital city**…' (10: 106 ff.)
'With what overwhelming sensations did I receive the tidings of **the fall of Robespierre** (July 27th, 1794), which was to change the colour of my life and give peace and consolation to so many millions of my fellow creatures!' (*Memoirs*, 85)	'O Friend! few happier moments have been mine / Through my whole life than that when first I heard / That this foul Tribe of Moloch was o'erthrown, / And their chief Regent levelled with the dust … / Great was my glee of spirit, great my joy / In vengeance, and eternal justice, thus made manifest' 10.466 ff and 539 ff
'And surely it was glorious to be a leader of the revolution; for, although **the sun of liberty**, like the orb of day when seen through opposing mists, has been turned into blood, its dawning beams were radiant, and it will again shake off the foul vapours that have hung around it, and spread that unsullied light which exhilarates all nature.' 2.2.23-4	**'Come now, ye golden times**… as the morning comes / From out the bosom of the night come ye' [10.541 ff 'And to the ultimate repose of things / I looked with unabated confidence [Frances's triumphs would be] … in the end / Great, universal, irresistible' [10. 577ff].

Williams:	Wordsworth:
On the summer of 1794: 'Louvet, Isnard, and others of our proscribed friends so long entombed in subterraneous dungeons ... now restored to society and to their country, recount to us the secrets of their prison house.' [Series 2 volume 4 welcomes the *return to constitutionality* and a bicameral legislature in 1795, as the achievement of these 'proscribed friends']]	'From this time forth,...Authority put on a milder face (10: 567) [and while rational experience could see] 'no shoots / And blossoms of a second spring' (1850: 11: 5–6) [and the senate's measures seemed] of heartless omen...In the people was my trust / And in the virtues which mine eyes had seen '(10: 577–8) '...I began / to think with fervour upon management of nations, what it is ought to be, / And how their worth depended on their Laws / And on the Constitution of the State' [10: 684 ff]
Nature: 'Upon the fall of Robespierre the terrible spell which bound the land of France was broken. The shrieking whirlwinds, the black precipices, the bottomless gulfs, suddenly vanished, and reviving nature covered the wastes with flowers and the rocks with verdure.... the waters are regaining their purity, are returning to their natural channels, and are no longer disturbed and sullied in their courses. 2.3.190 (and *Memoirs*, 192)	... 'To nature then, power had reverted' [10: 609–10 [Ambiguously situated. In context, the antecedent dawn is that which breaks in August 1794 upon the sands of Leven. But the next dateable reference is to 'open war' which began with British victory in Toulon in Aug 1793, when W was in the Isle of Wight watching the fleet assemble] '...Bliss was it in *that dawn* to be alive, / But to be young was very Heaven!' [10: 692–3]
On the Abbé Grégoire, Bishop of Blois: 'When terror was the order of the day, when atheism was the standard of republican principles, and when bishops, priests and even protestant minsters, in the convention, professed themselves the converts of Cloots the atheist and of Chaumette, the town-clerk of Paris; Gregoire with virtuous indignation boldly proclaimed his his belief in the doctrines of Christianity...' (2.4.4)	'A bishop [Gregoire], a man of philosophy and humanity as distinguished as your Lordship, declared at the opening of the national convention, and twenty-five millions of men were convinced of the truth of the assertion, that there was not a citizen on the tenth of august who, if he could have dragged before the eyes of Louis the corse of one of his murdered brothers, might not have exclaimed to him, Tyran, voilà ton ouvrage.' [*Llandaff*]

Williams:	Wordsworth:
Loyalty: 'the cause of liberty is not the less sacred, nor her charms less divine, because sanguinary monsters and sordid savages have defiled her temple...'(2.4.178)	'How could I believe / That wisdom could in any shape come near / Men clinging to delusions so insane?' [as those who thought France lost]; 10627 ff]]
On French victories in 1793–94: *'Imagination toils after victories like these.* Not four months had elapsed since the Austrians were almost within view of Paris ...What then in four short months has driven these mighty hosts from the frontiers of the republic? What has armed not only the young but has renovated the vigour of the old? What but that holy flame which liberty kindles in every heart but that of the base and degenerate?' (2.4.216-7)	[no one could resist their cause] 'Who was not lost, abandoned, selfish, proud, / Mean, miserable, wilfully depraved, / Hater perverse of equity and truth.' [and of Waterloo]: **'Imagination ne'er before content ...** stooped to the victory on that Belgic field achieved
Despair [1801] 'Alas, can no other offerings be made to liberty than those of human blood? Are we ever to be deceived in the object of our hope, *... is our philosophy false, and neither liberty or truth made for man?'* (*Sketches*, 1. 9)	Man, Wordsworth comes to feel, is mocked by possession of the 'lordly attributes of will and choice' (11: 306-320) or as Coleridge puts it in 'France: an Ode' [1798] *liberty is incompatible with 'forms of human power'*
On Jacobin spin-doctors: 'Away with the meek convulsions of revolutionary optimists, who ... tell us that although such events must be lamented, they are only transient blemishes in the grand drama of the revolution....I have not yet learnt to wipe away the bitter tears which fall for actual, positive miseries, by speculations of future probable good '(*Sketches* 1. 12-13)	[The closest remark in WW to this position, which is Simone de Beauvoir's argument in *The Ethics of Ambiguity*, belongs to the *Addresses to the Freeholders of Westmorland* I 1818]: where WW observes that it requires 'jacobinical infatuation' to sacrifice 'the near to the remote' (*PrW* 3: 170).

Williams:	Wordsworth:
On **Naples**: 'what overwhelmed the Neapolitan patriots with the most astonishment... was the sight of British officers employed in the execution of barbarous orders ... 'becoming satellites of the cruelty of the king of Naples' .... 'surely England will wipe away this vile, this degrading contamination' (*Sketches*, 1. 218)	'Lord Nelson['s] public life was stained with one great crime, so that ... I have not been able to connect his name with the poem ['The Happy Warrior'] as I could wish, or even to think of him with satisfaction in reference to the idea of what a warrior ought to be'. [*The Fenwick Notes* (Humanities-Ebooks 2007), 118, 302]
On Augean Stables: In 1794–95 the new 'legislative commissions are proceeding on the business of the state; the greater part of their occupations will be cleansing **the Augean stable** of the state of the most obnoxious of the forty thousand laws, which the industry of succeeding legislators had created ... [though] the most salutary water that can flow for the present, is that of oblivion' (*Sketches*, 2. 21.)	[c.f. WW's retrospective application of the image to 93–94 in *Prelude* 10: 546–8, looking back on] 'They who with clumsy desperation brought / Rivers of Blood, and preached that nothing else / Could cleanse **the Augean stable**...'
On **Napoleon 1802–04**: 'The rapid successive graduations to the consulate for life, and thence to the imperial purple, dispelled all illusion, and displayed the undisguised truth: Thou hast it now, King, Cawdor, Glamis, all...' *Narrative* [1816] 12	[*Vide*: the sonnets, esp. 'Calais, August 15 1802', and *Prelude* 10: 930 ff on the coronation:] 'when, finally... a Pope / Is summoned in to crown an Emperor; / This last opprobrium, when we see the dog / Returning to his vomit.... [the application of this biblical simile is initiated by Gilbert Wakefield, in *A Reply to Some Parts of the Bishop of Llandaff's Address to the People of Great Britain*, 1798, likening the mere possibility of France returning to monarchy as 'the dog returning to his vomit']

Williams:	Wordsworth:
On Wellington: '... he had met the vaunting con-queror of Europe at the head of the most formidable armies; he had laid his renowned legions in the dust; he had torn the imperial crown from his brow, and driven him from his usurped empire, the capital of which he was about to enter. The Duke of Wellington invites the French gen-erals to a conference; he leads them through his ranks; he displays his positions, his plans, his resources; he grants them the necessary time for deliberation: the sword is returned to its scabbard, and Paris is spared!' *Narrative*, 246–7	[There is no equivalent for this passage in Wordsworth, who refuses to adulate Wellington. He does ascribe Waterloo and its aftermath to 'magnanimity' but it is the virtue of the country as a whole, in the so-called 'Thanksgiving Ode', not of Wellington]
Aftermath [Thanks to its experiences, France has read] 'the table of contents of lib-eral principles, and they will at last comprehend the whole volume.... The spirit of constitutional represen-tation is abroad, and will walk the world.' *Narrative*, 305–7	[Whether WW is left with even so much residual optimism is perhaps debateable?]

SOME OTHER CONTRIBUTORY VOICES
Jean-Baptiste Louvet, *Narrative* [Joseph Johnson, 1795] 'I was compelled to acknowledge, that, of all kinds of slavery, that induced by anarchy is the most intolerable. When the ignorant and misguided multitude reigns, crimes are as numerous as masters. …Thus the guillotine becomes the national altar, to which brother will citizenly drive brother; or the father his son.' (70)
Mary Wollstonecraft, *An Historical and Moral View of the French Revolution* (1795), 299, 399–400. [Because] 'vanity had made every Frenchman a theorist' [it took the French unconscionably longer than it took the Americans to arrive at a viable constitution]: 'Such is the difference between men acting from practical knowledge, and men who are governed entirely by theory, or by no principle whatever'.
David Williams, *Regulations of Parochial Police,* London: J Owen, 1797. [BL tracts: 1042.1.30.4.] 'While Europe has been agitated to its utmost extremities by the contending interests and dispositions of [1] persons and parties, who would preserve its ancient institutions, even in their worst abuses—[2] of those who would gradually assimilate them to the gradual improvements of man—and [3] of those who would rapidly exchange them for the forms of fancy, or the faultless monsters of unexperienced philosophy, the institutions themselves have tottered…' (p. 5
[Anon]. *An Historical View of The French Revolution. From the Assembling of the States General in May 1789 to the acceptance of the Republican Constitution in September 1795.* 2 vols. Newcastle upon Tyne, 1796. '…in the subsequent parts of the historic narrative, the reader will find that the sacred cause of liberty remains unimpeached. These horrific extravagances did indeed form a black cloud, which for a time obscured the rising sun of liberty in that nation…' (viii)

Romanticism from Humanities-Ebooks

John Beer, Blake's Humanism

John Beer, Coleridge the Visionary

Jared Curtis, *The Cornell Wordsworth: a Supplement* †

Jared Curtis, ed. *The Fenwick Notes of William Wordsworth**

Jared Curtis, ed., *The Poems of William Wordsworth: Collected Reading Texts from the Cornell Wordsworth*, 3 vols.*

Richard Gravil, ed., *Master Narratives: Tellers and Telling in the English Novel. Essays for Bill Ruddick*

Richard Gravil and Molly Lefebure, eds, *The Coleridge Connection: Essays for Thomas McFarland*

Richard Gravil and W J B Owen, eds, *William Wordsworth: Concerning the Convention of Cintra**

Simon Hull, ed., *The British Periodical Text, 1796–1832*

W. J. B. Owen, *Understanding 'The Prelude'*

W. J. B. Owen and J. W. Smyser, eds, *Wordsworth's Political Writings**

W. J. B. Owen and J. W. Smyser, eds, *The Prose Works of William Wordsworth*, Volume 1*

Pamela Perkins, ed. *Francis Jeffrey: Highland and Continental Tours**

†Cloth *Paperback

http://www.humanities-ebooks.co.uk